PRAISE FOR A

CW01024540

'Everything a pony-mad girl wants and needs in a fabulous series of pony stories. Every time I read the latest book I think it's the best but Amanda has done it again.'

'Yet another fabulous Riverdale story!! Can't get enough of them!!!'

'A pony classic for the future.'

EDGE OF DANGER

AMANDA WILLS

Cherry Tree
Publishing

In memory of Anna Sewell, who encouraged kindness, sympathy, and understanding towards horses, yet never lived to see the impact of her legacy.

Poppy McKeever swung into the saddle, toed her feet into the stirrups and tightened Cloud's girth a notch. The Connemara tossed his dappled grey head and skittered sideways.

'Steady,' Poppy murmured, running a hand along his neck. 'Red's not going anywhere.'

She spied her stepmum on her knees in the vegetable garden, planting out a row of spindly leek seedlings. 'I'm off then,' she yelled. 'I'll be back before lunch.'

Caroline waved her trowel, sending a shower of peaty dirt into the air, and Poppy turned her pony towards the gate that led to the moor. She nudged him with her heels, and he broke into a trot, his neat ears pricked as he headed along the track towards her best friend's house.

There was no sign of Scarlett or her pony Red in their usual meeting place, so they rode through another gate into the farmyard. Meg, Scarlett's border collie, woofed a greeting and Scarlett's head appeared over Red's stable door.

'Sorry,' she called. 'Won't be a minute. I just need to tack up.'

Poppy jumped off Cloud and led him across the yard. Red whickered and the two ponies touched noses as Scarlett let herself out of the stable. There was a smudge of dirt on her cheek, and her auburn curls were tangled.

'Were you working this morning?' Poppy asked.

'No. I wanted to give Red a quick bath so I could get some photos.'

'What for?'

'My Instagram feed.'

'You're obsessed.'

Scarlett shrugged. 'Being an Instagram influencer takes time and effort, you know.'

Poppy raised an eyebrow. 'Is that what you are now, an Instagram influencer?'

'As of eight o'clock this morning, I have more than a thousand followers, actually. But I need at least double that.'

'Why?' Poppy enjoyed scrolling through the feeds of famous riders when she had nothing better to do, but Scarlett's current fixation with Instagram perplexed her.

'Because I want to be a brand ambassador and get loads of free stuff for Red and me. There's a girl I follow who hasn't bought a single thing for either herself or her horse for months. Companies are literally showering her with really cool gear.'

'Not literally,' Poppy corrected her. 'But it's such a time suck, all this faffing about taking arty pictures. I suppose you'll be wanting to stop every five minutes to take a photo on our hack. If we ever get going,' she added, as Scarlett whipped out her phone and snapped a shot of Red nuzzling Cloud's forelock.

'You'll be laughing on the other side of your face when LeMieux come knocking on my door offering me loads of new rugs and saddle pads just for posting pictures of Red wearing them.'

'I don't think it's quite as simple as that, Scar.'

'Where are we going?' Scarlett said, ignoring her.

'This one's so full of beans he could do with a good blast.' Poppy tweaked Cloud's ear. 'How about we head over towards Claydon? That lovely grassy track through the cornfields is perfect for a gallop.'

'As long as we don't bump into La-Di-Da Canning,' Scarlett said, pulling her stirrups down and ramming on her hat.

Poppy led Cloud over to the mounting block and jumped back on. 'Don't you mean Georgierideshorses?'

'Eh?'

'It's the name of Georgia's new Instagram account. She popped up on my feed the other day. Seems you're not the only one who wants to be a social media influencer.'

Scarlett muttered something under her breath. Poppy cocked her head, but the only words she caught were 'freeloader' and 'big-head'.

Scarlett was still grumbling to herself as they skirted the base of a small tor and joined the old railway track that led to Claydon Manor, the sprawling mansion Georgia's parents had bought a decade earlier with a massive lottery win.

'It's all right for Georgia, with her own personal riding instructor and the best jumping pony in the South West,' Scarlett groused.

'Angela's the livery yard manager now, and Georgia's parents bought her Barley before they spent all their money. According to Georgia they're flat broke these days,' Poppy said.

Scarlett snorted. 'Hardly. They still live in that socking great house with an indoor arena, a horse walker and a solarium, don't they? Whereas we...'

'We what?'

'Nothing.' She bit her lip and gazed at the horizon.

Poppy swung around in her saddle to face her. 'What's up, Scar?'

She was silent for a moment as she played with a hank of Red's mane. 'I heard Mum and Dad talking last night. They're worried about money. It's been so dry the spring barley hasn't germinated, *and* the grass isn't growing so they're having to buy in silage for the cattle. And if that wasn't bad enough, the beef prices are terrible. My wages pay for Red's shoes and feed, but there's never anything left over for nice things for him. Or me for that matter.'

Poppy knew she was lucky - her dad and Caroline paid for Cloud's upkeep, and she saved up her birthday and Christmas money for anything else she needed.

Suddenly everything made sense. 'Is that what this Instagram craze is really about?'

Scarlett's head bobbed up and down. 'The inter-schools showjumping competition begins next term, and we can't go looking like this.' She tugged a loose thread on Red's faded blue saddle pad, and a piece of the edging came away in her hand. 'Everything we have is third-hand and falling apart. But there's no way I can ask Mum and Dad for a posh new saddle pad when they're struggling to afford to feed the cows.'

'I'd forgotten the first round was coming up,' said Poppy, who hadn't made the team. 'You can borrow my white saddle pad if you like. It'd look great on Red. And I'll lend you my show jacket.'

Scarlett gave her the briefest of smiles. 'That's really kind, and I appreciate it, but for once I'd like my own nice things, you know? That's why I need more followers. Because if I can get companies to give me stuff for free, I wouldn't need to worry about asking Mum and Dad.'

———

THEY REACHED THE BROAD, grassy track and gave the ponies their heads. The wind whipped colour into Poppy's cheeks and ruffled Cloud's mane as he matched Red stride for stride. Beside her, Scarlett held her reins in one hand as she fiddled about in her coat pocket.

'Everything OK?' Poppy called.

'Fine.' Scarlett produced her phone, her reins slipping through her fingers as she started pressing furiously. 'I just want to record a quick video of us galloping.'

'Is that a good idea?'

'You're such a worrier. It'll be fine. Just chill,' Scarlett said.

Poppy gave a little shake of her head and squeezed her reins. With Scarlett risking a one-handed gallop, it would be prudent to slow down.

'Don't say anything. I'm filming… now!' Scarlett shouted over the drumming of the ponies' hooves and the roar of the wind.

Red, realising his mistress's mind was elsewhere, stretched out his neck and quickened his pace until his chestnut legs were a blur. Cloud, not wanting to be left behind, surged forwards. So much for a sensible pace, Poppy thought, crouching low over her pony's neck.

Scarlett was holding the reins in one hand and her phone in the other as she panned from Cloud to Red and back again. As relaxed in the saddle as a cowgirl, she was beaming from ear to ear. It was the happiest Poppy had seen her all morning.

Just chill, Scarlett had said. *You're such a worrier*. It was true. Poppy was cautious by nature, always had been. Perhaps it had something to do with the fact that her mum had died when she was four. She knew how quickly fate could deal a cruel hand.

As they galloped towards the skyline, Poppy decided to lighten up. If Scarlett wanted to be an Instagram influencer, then who was she to rain on her parade? One of the things Poppy loved about her best friend was that she always embraced new experiences, unlike Poppy, who could see the pitfalls in everything.

But this Easter holidays Poppy would throw caution to the wind. She'd be positive and would say yes if new opportunities came her way. She'd be less Poppy, more Scarlett.

A cock pheasant shot out of the corn to their right, an explosion of flapping russet and bronze feathers. The bird's alarm call cut through the thrumming of the ponies' hooves, as piercing as a klaxon.

Several things happened at once. Red threw his head up in horror and veered to the left, almost colliding with Cloud. Poppy grabbed a handful of Cloud's mane and tugged on her reins. Scarlett, still riding one-handed, cried out as her mobile flew into the air and landed on the track with a crunch. Red, spying the flying phone out of the corner of his eye, spooked again, twisting his body into a rodeo buck and throwing Scarlett out of the saddle. She teetered in midair for a second, shrieked, and tumbled to the ground.

2

The whites of Red's eyes were showing, and his nostrils were flared as he galloped on. With every stride the stirrups banged against his flanks, increasing his panic. Poppy clamped her legs to Cloud's sides and urged him towards the chestnut gelding. As they drew alongside Red, she leaned forwards as far as she could, her arm outstretched.

'Steady, boy,' she soothed as she reached for Red's reins. He flicked an ear back, and his pace faltered. 'That's right, easy does it.' Poppy's fingers were centimetres from Red's reins. She tilted forwards and tried to catch them, but her fingers closed around thin air. She swiped at them a second time and missed again.

Poppy slumped in the saddle. They were fast approaching the brow of the hill. After that, just one cornfield separated them from the road that led to Claydon Manor. And if she couldn't catch Red before he reached the road...

Straightening her shoulders, Poppy took a deep breath and stood in her stirrups. She lunged for the reins, gasping with relief as her hand closed around the slippery leather. Clasping it firmly, she murmured, 'I've got you now, kiddo.' Red cantered for a few paces, then dropped down to a trot. 'And *walk*.' She stretched out the word so the cadence matched the slower pace. Red's ear flicked back again, and he slowed to a walk. Poppy closed her eyes and sucked in air, trying to steady her racing heartbeat.

She jumped off and checked both ponies over. Their necks were dark with sweat and their flanks were heaving, but otherwise they seemed fine. She scoured the track, half expecting to see Scarlett jogging up the hill towards them, but it was deserted. Even the pheasant had long gone.

'Scarlett!' Poppy yelled. But there was no answer. With a growing sense of unease, Poppy led the ponies back down the hill.

SHE FOUND Scarlett sitting on the track close to where the pheasant had flown out of the corn. She was hugging her knees to her chest and groaning.

'Are you all right?'

Scarlett lifted a tear-streaked face to Poppy's and shook her head. 'It's broken.'

'Oh no!' Poppy looped the ponies' reins over her arm and reached for her phone. 'I'll call an ambulance. Is it your collarbone?'

Scarlett rubbed her face with her hands. 'What?'

'Is it your collarbone that's broken?'

Scarlett frowned. 'No, my phone. I've smashed the screen. Look.' She held it out. A spider's web of shattered glass covered the screen.

'But you're all right?' Poppy said.

Scarlett jumped to her feet. 'I'm fine.'

Poppy handed her Red's reins. 'And Red's fine. That's the main thing, isn't it?'

'Not really. I can't afford a new screen, and it's not insured. And without my phone I can't do Instagram, and without Instagram I can't become a brand ambassador. And if I can't become a brand ambassador I can't get Red new things.' She narrowed her eyes at her pony, who was standing serenely as if butter wouldn't melt. 'Not that you deserve anything after turfing me off, you horror.'

'I'll lend you the money to get it fixed,' Poppy said.

Scarlett gave her the ghost of a smile. 'But I'd have to pay you back about fifty pence a week for the next two years.'

Poppy giggled, then turned serious. 'I wouldn't mind.'

'I know.' Scarlett sighed, zipped her broken phone into the pocket of her coat and hauled herself into the saddle. 'But I'd rather earn the money myself.'

They headed back up the track at a walk this time, even though the pheasant was long gone. To take Scarlett's mind off her phone, Poppy quizzed her about the school showjumping team's latest training session.

'Mrs Jackson set up a course with some scary fillers

and two doubles. Red was jumping his little white socks off. Mrs Jackson wants us to go first to put the wind up the competition.' Scarlett grinned. 'Princess Georgia wasn't too impressed with *that*, as you can imagine.'

'I bet.' Poppy cocked her head. A distant rumble reverberated around the valley. 'Is that a car?'

'Sounds more like a lorry. Let's pull into Princess Georgia's drive to let it pass. I don't want Red spooking again.'

They trotted up to Claydon Manor's imposing wrought iron gates and waited. A huge articulated truck appeared around the corner of the lane and stopped. The driver flicked on the hazard lights and wound down his window.

'It's OK,' Poppy called, waving him on. 'The ponies are fine with traffic.'

He jumped down from the cab and came around to the front of the vehicle, scratching his head. 'We're looking for Claydon Manor.'

'Then you've found it,' said Scarlett, pointing to the slate sign set into the stone wall. 'There's a keypad here. You have to press the key with the bell on it,' she added.

The driver nodded his thanks, but before he'd even reached the keypad the electronic gates started swinging open. He frowned.

'CCTV,' Poppy said, pointing to the small camera on top of one of the gateposts. 'Seems like they were expecting you.'

'Seems like they were,' he agreed, jumping back into the cab. The two girls steered their ponies out of the way and the truck chugged past. It was cherry red with a large white logo on its side, shaped like a video camera.

'See Red Productions,' Poppy read.

Cloud fidgeted as another three identical trucks drove in. Just when Poppy thought that was it, a pair of black lorries turned into the drive. They bore a different logo - two swirly silver Ks with the words, 'The difference between ordinary and extraordinary' sign-written underneath.

'Hey, those last two were horse lorries, weren't they?' Scarlett said, craning her neck to get a better look.

'They did look like it,' Poppy agreed. 'But who are See Red Productions, and what, more importantly, are they doing at Claydon Manor?'

3

Poppy and Scarlett watched the small procession of lorries trundle down the sweeping drive to the front of the Cannings' beautiful home. When they peeled off to the right and disappeared around the back of the house Poppy unzipped her pocket.

'I'll text Georgia and ask what's going on.'

Scarlett wheeled Red around. 'No, don't give Her Royal Highness the satisfaction of knowing we care.'

'Her Royal Highness? That's a new one. I know you two are never going to be best buddies, but it would be nice if you could suspend hostilities once in a while, especially as you're both on the school showjumping team,' Poppy said. 'How does Mrs Jackson cope with you sniping at each other all the time?'

'She did tell us we needed to bury the hatchet at our last training session,' Scarlett admitted. 'Preferably not in each other's backs.'

Poppy smothered a giggle.

'But she's just so unbearably smug, and supercilious, and, oh I don't know, she just rubs me up the wrong way.'

'Because you let her,' Poppy said. 'So you don't want to know what See Red Productions is doing at the Cannings' place?'

Scarlett stuck her nose in the air. 'I really couldn't care less.'

POPPY WAS CURIOUS, though, and once they were home and she'd turned Cloud out into the paddock he shared with their donkeys Chester and Jenny, she took the family laptop up to her bedroom and googled them.

'See Red Productions is an award-winning, London-based independent television and film production company that specialises in family entertainment,' she told Magpie, who was curled in a ball at the end of her bed. 'They work with the finest talent to acquire, develop and produce hit feature films and television series.'

Her brother Charlie bounded into the room. 'Talking to yourself is the first sign of madness,' he said.

'Thanks for the tip, but I was talking to Magpie if you must know.'

'Talking to cats is the second… actually, talking to cats is fine. I do it all the time.' He grinned, tickled Magpie's chin and sat beside her. 'What were you telling him?'

'We saw a load of lorries arriving at Claydon Manor

this morning. You know, Georgia Canning's place? They were from a company called See Red Productions. I was looking them up. They make television programmes.'

'Cool. D'you think they're making a programme about Georgia?'

'I wouldn't have thought so. But why else would they be there?'

'Why don't you ask her when you see her at school tomorrow?'

Poppy closed the laptop and slid it onto her bedside table. 'I will.'

———

SCARLETT SPENT the journey to school the next morning thinking of ways to earn some extra cash.

'Barney's given me a few extra hours at the shop, but a new screen's going to cost fifty quid. It'll take me ages to save up enough.'

'What about babysitting? You could put a postcard up in the shop window,' Poppy said.

'I guess.'

'Or see if Bella needs a hand mucking out at Redhall.'

'I suppose I could ask.'

'Can you still use your phone?'

'Just about. Alex had a spare screen protector, so I've stuck that on. But selfies aren't exactly professional through cracked glass. It's a total disaster.'

The bus pulled into the layby outside their school,

and the two girls stepped off. As they crossed the road Poppy spied Georgia Canning and her best friend Fiona Cavanagh-Smythe passing through the school gates.

'Hey, Georgia!' Poppy called. 'Wait a minute.'

The older girl stopped, and Poppy grabbed Scarlett's arm and dragged her over.

'Well, if it isn't Poppy McKeever and her sidekick Scarlett Chapman.' Georgia peered at Scarlett. 'What's up? Did the wind change direction while you were eating a lemon?'

Scarlett scowled and was about to retort when Poppy butted in.

'We were riding past your place yesterday and saw the television production company arrive. What are they doing there?'

Georgia's lip curled into a sneer. 'What business is it of yours?'

'It's not. We just wondered, didn't we, Scar?'

'Yeah, we thought they might be filming the new series of Brat Camp.'

Georgia fixed her flinty blue eyes on Scarlett. 'Very funny. Actually, I'm surprised you haven't heard. They're on location at ours for a couple of weeks.'

Scarlett gaped. 'You mean they're filming there over the Easter holidays?'

'That's what being on location means, yes.'

'What are they filming?' Poppy asked.

Georgia flicked her hair back. 'A re-make of Black Beauty. The location scout saw our house in an old edition of Country Life and thought it would be perfect as Birtwick Park. That's Squire Gordon's house,' she added, looking down her nose at Scarlett.

A flush crept up Scarlett's neck. 'I have read Black Beauty.'

'That's why there were two horseboxes,' Poppy said.

'We're stabling their horses while they're filming. They have their own horse trainer and stunt rider. And Fiona and I are going to be extras. They're paying us fifty pounds a day.'

'Fifty pounds *and* you get to be on the telly?' Scarlett's eyes were wide.

For a moment, there was a crack in Georgia's haughty exterior, and she grinned. 'I know, it's pretty cool, right? They're looking for more extras for a village scene they're shooting this weekend. Why don't you come over tomorrow morning to see if they want you, too?'

'SHALL WE GO?' Poppy said as they headed for their form room.

Scarlett chewed her lip. 'I could earn enough to pay for a new screen for my phone in one day. And it does sound fun.'

'It does,' Poppy agreed.

'But I hate the thought of being beholden to Georgia.'

'She isn't as bad as you make out. Think of it as a bonding experience. A way of burying the hatchet before your next jumping session with Mrs Jackson. And we don't have anything else planned for this weekend, do we?'

'No, but…'

Poppy remembered her resolution to say yes to new opportunities. 'I'm going to give it a go even if you don't,' she said, linking arms with Scarlett. 'But it would be more fun if you came, too. You can earn enough to have your phone mended, take loads of really cool photos of the set and you'll be a brand ambassador in no time.'

'You're right,' Scarlett said. 'It's a no brainer. Who cares about Georgia? Birtwick Park here we come!'

4

Butterflies danced in Poppy's stomach as she followed Scarlett up the Claydon drive the following day. She'd dressed in her best jeans and her favourite sweatshirt, and Caroline had plaited her hair in a French braid. Poppy didn't know why, but it had seemed more appropriate than her usual ponytail.

She'd spent a couple of hours the previous evening flicking through her well-thumbed copy of Black Beauty, re-reading snippets.

'Did you know that Anna Sewell wrote Black Beauty almost one hundred and fifty years ago?' she told Scarlett. 'It was the only novel she wrote, and she died five months after it was published. How sad is that?'

'Really sad,' Scarlett said. 'Can I borrow your mobile for a selfie?'

Poppy handed Scarlett her phone. 'And fifty million

copies have been sold since then. It's one of the best-selling books of all time.'

'I'll just AirDrop this to my phone if that's OK?'

'Go ahead. Anna Sewell said she wrote the book to...' Poppy tried to remember the exact words. '"To induce kindness, sympathy, and an understanding treatment of horses." It's been described as the most influential anti-cruelty novel of all time.'

'Crikey,' Scarlett said. 'Can you take a photo of me? I want to be pointing at the house with both hands, but I can't do that and hold the phone.'

'Sure,' Poppy said, taking the phone back. 'Say cheese.'

'Sausages works better for me. Makes me look more natural.' She smoothed her hair and gazed at the camera. 'Sausages.'

Poppy snapped away. 'Thanks to Anna Sewell, they banned the bearing rein.'

'The what?' Scarlett asked, a fixed grin on her face.

'It's a strap they used to keep carriage horses' heads high even though it damaged their necks. It was fashionable back then, apparently.' She shivered. Black Beauty's plight as a carriage horse in Victorian London made for an uncomfortable read. 'Thank goodness no-one has to treat horses like that any more.' She showed Scarlett the pictures she'd taken. 'Are they OK?'

'Cool, thanks,' Scarlett said. 'How d'you know all this stuff, anyway?'

Poppy shuffled her feet. 'I decided to mug up on the book in case the director asked me any questions.'

Scarlett snorted. 'It's not a job interview.'

'But what if we have to audition? Have you prepared a piece?'

A flicker of doubt crossed Scarlett's face. 'No, but we're just going to be standing around in the background, aren't we? Why would you need to audition for that?'

'Well, I memorised the scene where Black Beauty meets Merrylegs just in case.'

Scarlett elbowed her in the ribs. 'Swot.'

'There's nothing wrong with being prepared.'

'If you say so. I wonder if anyone famous is in it.'

They stopped outside Claydon's imposing front door. Poppy took a deep breath and reached for the ornate door pull. 'I guess we're about to find out.'

THE DOOR WAS OPENED by Angela Snell, the hook-nosed harridan who had once been Georgia's riding instructor but now ran the livery yard at Claydon.

'Here for the filming?' she barked.

The two girls nodded.

'Head straight through the house. You'll find the circus camped out in the field behind the outdoor manege.'

'Circus?' whispered Scarlett as they tip-toed down the wood-panelled hallway.

'I expect she's talking about the film crew,' Poppy whispered back. 'I can't imagine Angela taking too kindly to them moving in, can you? She probably thinks it's all a bit beneath her.'

Her eyes roved back and forth as she followed Scarlett through the manor house. Poppy had been struck by how threadbare it had been the last time she'd been inside. It looked even shabbier now. Cobwebs adorned the dark, dusty portraits that lined the walls and a rotting floorboard had been pulled up and abandoned against a radiator. A faint fusty smell lingered beneath the scent of beeswax. Poppy glanced at the portraits as they passed. With their raven-black hair and piercing blue eyes, the stony-faced subjects could have passed for Georgia's haughty ancestors. But Georgia's mum used to work in a supermarket, her dad was a builder, and their home had been a three bedroomed semi before their lottery win. They'd burnt through their fortune and now Claydon Manor, in all its faded Georgian glory, was all they had left.

Poppy and Scarlett reached the boot room at the back of the house, let themselves out of the back door and were halfway across the stable yard when Georgia appeared.

'Come and meet Peggy, the casting director,' she said, without preamble. 'I told her you were coming. She'll explain everything.'

'Have they started filming already?' Poppy asked.

Georgia nodded. 'They've just stopped for a break. They were up early filming Black Beauty galloping across the moor while the sun was rising behind him. It's for the opening credits.'

'Wow. What's Black Beauty like?'

'Follow me, and I'll show you,' Georgia said. She turned on her heels and strode across to a row of loose boxes. A bright bay hunter appeared over the top of the stable door and whickered.

'That's Sir Oliver,' Georgia said. 'Although his real name is Brian. He's a poppet.'

Poppy peeled off a Polo from the packet in her pocket and held it on an outstretched hand. The gelding nibbled it daintily, his whiskers tickling her wrist. She rubbed his forelock as he crunched the Polo.

Scarlett was staring into his stable with a horrified expression on her face.

'What's wrong?'

'His tail's docked,' she hissed.

Poppy frowned. 'Are you sure? I thought docking was illegal.'

'It is,' Scarlett said, sliding the bolt across. 'I'm going to take a proper look.'

'Don't,' Georgia said, placing a hand on Scarlett's arm. 'Krystal doesn't like anyone going into the horses' stables.'

'Who the heck is Krystal?' Poppy said.

'Krystal King, the horse trainer. Surely you've heard of her? She trains horses for all the big films. She's amazing.'

'I wouldn't call docking horses' tails amazing. I'd call it downright cruel,' Scarlett retorted.

'Calm down. His tail's not docked, Krystal's just trimmed it short for the filming. Sir Oliver's tail in the book was docked, you see.' Georgia graced them with a patronising smile.

'He was sad because he couldn't swish the flies away,' Poppy remembered.

'And there aren't any flies at the moment, so it's not a problem, is it? Come and say hello to Black Beauty. His real name's Isadore.'

At the sound of his name, a handsome black horse with a glossy, flowing mane poked his head over the stable door.

'Wow,' breathed Scarlett.

'Beautiful, isn't he? He's an eight-year-old Friesian stallion. Krystal imported him from the Netherlands last autumn. She's been training him for this role ever since. She's promised me a ride on him when they've finished filming.'

The stallion tossed his head. Everything about him, from his high head carriage to his regal demeanour, screamed presence.

'He's a perfect Black Beauty,' Poppy said.

'Ginger, aka Roxie, is in the stable next door. But be careful. She's as bad-tempered as the real Ginger. She bit the stunt rider yesterday and drew blood.'

Keeping their distance, Poppy and Scarlett peered into the loose box. All they could see was an elegant chestnut rump.

'I'd call her over, but she'd probably bite me, too,' Georgia said in an undertone.

'Ginger was only feisty because people had mistreated her,' Poppy said.

'I'd never buy a chestnut mare. Everyone knows they're fickle and difficult,' Georgia said, looking side-long at Scarlett.

'You're talking a load of rubbish,' Scarlett snapped.

'Blaze is chestnut, and she's the sweetest mare there ever was.'

'I'm assuming Merrylegs is in the last stable?' Poppy interrupted.

A mischievous smile crept across Georgia's face. 'Ah, yes, Merrylegs. The little grey pony that Squire Gordon's daughters ride. Why don't you take a look, Poppy?'

She stepped out of the way, and Poppy looked into the last stable. Expecting to find a wide-girthed Welsh Mountain Pony or even a portly Shetland, she stepped back in surprise.

Because dozing at the back of the stable, his head low and his rump facing them, was Cloud.

5

P oppy's mouth fell open. She blinked once, twice, then stared back into the stable. Cloud was still there, his dappled grey coat lit by a shaft of sunlight as he slept. But it wasn't possible. Poppy had left her grass-stained pony grazing in the paddock at home with Jenny and Chester. How had someone managed to shampoo him until his coat shone silver, then whisk him here under her nose? She tugged at the neck of her sweatshirt and finally found her voice.

'Cloud?'

He didn't move a muscle. 'Cloud?' she said again. 'It's me, Poppy.' Still no reaction. It was as if he'd been frozen in time and her heart clenched.

Scarlett shot her a puzzled look. 'What did you say?'

Poppy pointed into the stable and cleared her throat. 'It's Cloud,' she croaked.

'Cloud? But what's he doing here?'

'It isn't Cloud,' Georgia said. 'Looks like him though, doesn't he?'

Scarlett elbowed Poppy out of the way. 'Crikey, I see what you mean.' She clicked her tongue and the straw rustled. A nose appeared over the stable door. A nose that was the delicate pink of a newborn baby, not seal-grey like Cloud's. Georgia was right, it wasn't him after all. The tightness in Poppy's chest loosened.

'His real name's Perry,' Georgia said. 'He's a Connemara, too.'

Poppy couldn't take her eyes off him. Apart from the muzzle, he was Cloud's double, from his iron-grey points to his neat little ears. The likeness was uncanny. She pulled another Polo out of the packet and held it in the palm of her hand. Perry eyed her warily. He seemed to be deliberating whether she was friend or foe. All of a sudden Poppy was transported back to a clearing in the Riverdale woods, her hand clasped around a bucket of pony nuts as she tried to win the trust of a half-wild pony running free on the moor.

'It's OK, I won't bite,' she whispered. Perry inched forwards and, deciding Poppy wasn't a threat, stretched out his neck and hoovered up the Polo.

'He looks a lot like Cloud, but he doesn't look much like Merrylegs. He was short and round and about twelve hands high, wasn't he?' Scarlett said.

'They needed him to be bigger because Squire Gordon's daughters, Flora and Jessie, are about our age in this adaption,' Georgia said. She dipped her head. 'We should find Peggy.'

Poppy cast one look back at Cloud's double and followed Georgia towards the film set.

PEGGY WAS a cheerful woman about Caroline's age who had a pen tucked behind her ear and a clipboard clasped to her chest.

'Let's have a good look at you,' she said.

Poppy stood with her legs braced and stuffed her hands into her pockets, then pulled them out again. She rubbed the back of her neck, then left her arms dangling by her sides. The Dartmoor ponies must feel like this when they arrived at the auctions, fresh off the moor. Under scrutiny. Should she smile? Share some of her best Black Beauty facts? Perhaps she should mention her walk-on part in the school's panto the previous Christmas. Peggy didn't need to know that she'd stuttered over her only line.

Before she could decide, Peggy scribbled something on her clipboard. 'You,' she said, pointing her pen at Poppy. 'You can be one of the schoolchildren. And you,' she turned to Scarlett, 'have the ruddy look of a domestic about you. You can be one of Squire Gordon's scullery maids.'

Georgia barked with laughter.

'Thanks very much,' Scarlett said.

If Peggy detected the sarcasm in Scarlett's voice, she ignored it. 'Please see Anoushka in wardrobe, and she'll sort out your costumes. Kelvin, the assistant director,' she nodded towards an angular man in jeans and a white teeshirt who was staring into the back of a camera, 'will let you know what he wants you to do. Filming starts in twenty minutes.'

GEORGIA WAS STILL CHUCKLING as they went in search of Anoushka.

'"The ruddy look of a domestic." I couldn't have put it better myself. Of course, I'm a schoolchild, too.'

'Bully for you,' Scarlett said. Her face was growing redder and redder, and Poppy knew it was only a matter of time before she blew.

'Oh look, there's Fiona,' Poppy said, hoping to distract her.

Georgia's best friend was standing outside one of the trailers, dressed in a teal-blue bodice, long skirt, straw hat and leather boots. A woman with a tape measure around her neck was pinning the hem of the skirt. She saw the three girls and beckoned them over.

'Extras?' she asked through a mouthful of pins.

Georgia nodded. 'Two more schoolchildren and one ruddy-faced scullery maid.'

Scarlett muttered something under her breath.

'Maids' uniforms are on the right, and the school-girls' outfits are on the left. Find one in your size, pop it on and come out and show me, please,' Anoushka said.

Stepping into the trailer, Poppy gasped. 'This is like the best fancy dress box ever,' she said, trailing her hand down the rails of costumes. There were enough outfits to kit out a hundred people. Silk dresses with enormous bustles; frock coats and morning coats; corsets and petticoats; breeches and cravats.

On shelves above the rails dozens of hats, from top hats and bowler hats to straw boaters and bonnets, were balanced precariously on top of each other. Box upon box of boots and shoes were tucked underneath.

'You should wear this one, Poppy. It matches your eyes,' Georgia said, handing Poppy an emerald-green bodice and skirt. She picked one the colour of ripe plums for herself. Scarlett glared at a rail of mono-chrome clothes. Inspecting the sizes on the hangers, she half-heartedly pulled out a black dress with a large white apron and a pair of thick black tights.

'Don't forget your hat,' Georgia said, dropping a lace mop cap on Scarlett's auburn curls and laughing. 'It suits you.' She grabbed Poppy's elbow. 'Come on, Poppy, let's get changed.'

As Poppy allowed Georgia to drag her towards the changing room at the far end of the trailer, she stole a glance at Scarlett. The flush on her best friend's cheeks had faded, and her face was now white with anger.

'Think of the money,' Poppy mouthed, rubbing her finger and thumb together.

Scarlett turned her back to Poppy and pulled the black dress over her teeshirt so savagely it almost ripped.

POPPY GAZED SURREPTITIOUSLY at her fellow extras as

Kelvin, the assistant director, briefed them. There were around a dozen of them, from smartly-dressed Victorian gentlemen in frock coats to street urchins shivering in rags. She almost envied them. Her own costume felt tight and restrictive. No wonder young ladies rode side-saddle in Victorian times. Give her a pair of jodhpurs and a sweater any day of the week.

Beside her, Scarlett was still silently fuming. When Poppy had offered to take her photo for Instagram, Scarlett had bitten her head off.

'You think I'd want anyone to see me in *this*?' she'd growled, picking up the end of her apron and dropping it again in disgust. 'Playing a skivvy's not going to help me become a brand ambassador, is it?'

'Probably not, but it's fun, isn't it?'

'If you say so.'

Kelvin snapped his clapperboard shut to grab everyone's attention.

'Welcome to the set of Black Beauty. For those of you who don't know, our adaption of Anna Sewell's classic story will be shown on BBC 1 as a six-part Sunday night drama next spring. Do we have any first-timers?'

Around half, including Poppy and Scarlett, held up their hands.

'As supporting artistes,' his eyes roved around the extras, 'your job is to help set the scene. You are human props; a walking background, if you like.'

'Charming,' Scarlett muttered.

Kelvin fixed her with a steely gaze. 'You are not being paid to talk. Don't say anything during a take, and don't talk between takes, either. Most importantly of all, don't talk to the actors. Meals are provided, but actors and crew have priority. Portaloos are over there. This morning we're filming the scene where Squire Gordon is called up to London on urgent business, and he's robbed by a gang of highwaymen.' Kelvin touched his nose and pointed to two men in their early twenties wearing black cloaks. 'You two, come with me. We won't need the rest of you until this afternoon.'

6

'I can't remember there being any highwaymen in Black Beauty,' Fiona said, as Kelvin and the two Dick Turpin lookalikes marched off.

'That's because there weren't any,' Poppy told her.

'Nothing wrong with a bit of creative licence,' Georgia said with a shrug. 'Fiona and I are going to grab something to eat at ours while we wait. You coming?'

Poppy felt Scarlett stiffen beside her, and she shook her head. 'You're all right, thanks. We don't mind hanging about here, do we Scar?'

'Suit yourself,' Georgia said.

'She's seriously getting on my nerves,' Scarlett said once they'd gone. 'Lording it up just because she knows everyone and we don't. And how come I end up in this terrible maid's costume while the three of you get to pose around in posh frocks?'

'It's really uncomfortable,' Poppy said, pulling at the

neck. 'At least yours is nice and loose. Shall we go and watch them filming?'

'Might as well.'

They joined the end of a trickle of people heading across the Claydon paddocks to a gate in the dry stone wall that led to the open moor. They scurried through and on the other side stopped and stared at the scene before them.

'Wow,' Poppy said. 'This is amazing.'

She had seen behind-the-scenes television programmes before, but the sheer intensity of the set took her breath away. Little tableaus were playing out everywhere she looked. Kelvin's head was bobbing like a buoy in choppy waters as he received instructions from an older man with slicked-back hair who was holding a megaphone. The director, Poppy guessed. A woman holding a large canvas bag passed pistols, masks and wigs to the two highwaymen. An actor in a frock coat and top hat had pinched the director's chair while a make-up girl dusted powder onto his face with a brush.

But Poppy's eyes were drawn to a carriage that was rumbling down the track towards them, pulled by two horses - one black, one chestnut. She clutched Scarlett's arm. 'Look, Black Beauty and Ginger!'

'Isadore and Roxie,' Scarlett corrected her. 'At least they look authentic.'

The carriage slithered to a halt and a boy wearing jodhpurs and a black polo shirt with the same silver logo as the two horse boxes jumped down. He said something to the director before loping towards a woman in a wheelchair who was holding the reins of three dark bay horses standing obediently by her side. The boy led two of the horses to the waiting highwaymen and helped them into the saddles, checking stirrup leathers and girths.

He sauntered back to the woman in the wheelchair, took the carrier bag hanging from the handle of the chair and deposited the contents on the grass. He peeled off his clothes to his underwear and pulled on a pair of breeches, a black smock shirt and a highwayman's cloak, hat and mask. Vaulting onto the third horse from a standstill, he wheeled her around and galloped up the hill, his fellow highwaymen on his tail.

'Did you see that?' Scarlett was aghast. 'That mare must be at least sixteen two, and he vaulted straight on.'

'Perhaps he's a stunt rider,' Poppy said. Her gaze was drawn to the woman in the wheelchair. Her hair was the colour of white gold, and it glinted in the spring sunshine as she wheeled her chair to the carriage.

Scarlett caught the eye of a harassed-looking runner who was carrying a tray of take-out coffee cups to the crew. 'Is it OK if we watch?'

'As long as you stay out of the way.' His eyes scanned the set. 'Sit on the wall. You'll be out of shot there. But remember not to make a sound when we start filming.'

They settled themselves on the wall, fanning their skirts around them. The actor in the frock coat and top hat climbed into the carriage, followed by a second actor wearing a bowler hat and a waistcoat. He picked up the reins, his eyes on Krystal.

'She's telling them how to drive the carriage,' Scarlett said out of the corner of her mouth.

'They must be Squire Gordon and his coachman John Manly,' Poppy whispered back.

The director held the megaphone to his lips. 'Everyone at their stations, please.' The crew scurried away, leaving just the horse-drawn carriage on set. The camera operators and sound technicians made last-minute adjustments to their equipment.

'Quiet on set! Roll sound.'

A man Poppy presumed must be the sound recordist gave the director the thumbs up.

'Roll camera!'

The cameraman gave a brief nod.

'Scene twenty-three, take one,' Kelvin, the assistant director, said. The clapperboard closed with a crack.

The cameraman tweaked the focus of his camera and, training it on the carriage, called out, 'Set'.

Poppy felt the hairs on the back of her neck stand up as the director raised the megaphone to his lips one more time.

'And... action!'

The actor playing John Manly picked up the whip in his right hand and the reins in his left, and clicked his tongue. The two horses broke into a trot, their hooves clattering on the stony track. After a while, Scarlett prodded Poppy's arm and pointed to the tor behind the carriage. Poppy cocked her head, her hand cupped around her ear. There it was - the rumble of hooves in the distance, growing louder as every second passed.

Then, suddenly, the three highwaymen on their bay horses galloped over the brow of the hill and thundered towards the horse-drawn carriage. Black Beauty whinnied in terror as they circled it like crows mobbing a kestrel. Squire Gordon shouted at his coachman to "ride like the wind". The actor's bowler hat flew off as he cracked the whip and Black Beauty and Ginger plunged forwards, their ears back and their nostrils flaring.

Poppy found herself leaning back on the dry stone wall, her heels digging into the ground, as the carriage pitched forwards. Galloping alongside the two horses, the highwaymen waved their pistols and fired shots into the sky.

Ginger squealed and barged into Black Beauty. The sudden movement caused the carriage to lurch to one side, and for a heart-stopping moment, the two offside wheels left the ground.

It's just a stunt, Poppy reminded herself. Everything will have been planned down to the smallest detail. The highwayman who'd vaulted on turned his horse on a sixpence and galloped to the other side of the carriage. Leaning forwards until he was almost horizontal, he pushed it back onto all four wheels then knotted his horse's reins and jumped into a standing position on the saddle.

Galloping neck and neck with Black Beauty, he leapt across to the black horse's back. With the pistol trained on Squire Gordon's chest, he grabbed the reins with his left hand and pulled the horses to a standstill.

'Stand and deliver!' he cried. 'Your life or your money!'

'Cut!' the director yelled, waving his arm at the camera and sound men. 'It's your money or your life, idiot boy!' he screeched at the stunt rider. 'Right, back to your stations, everyone, and we'll go again from the beginning.' He clicked his fingers at the stunt rider. 'Five simple words in the right order, that's all I'm asking for. Your money or your life. Got that?'

'Your money or your life,' the boy repeated in a sullen voice. He slithered down from Black Beauty and took the bay mare's reins from a member of the production team.

The second take was going well until John Manly dropped his whip when the highwaymen appeared. The third take seemed perfect to Poppy and Scarlett, but the director pronounced the lighting lacklustre.

By the fourth take they were growing fidgety.

'It's a bit boring, isn't it, watching the same scene over and over again?' Scarlett said.

'A bit like Groundhog Day,' Poppy agreed. 'Shall we find something to eat? My stomach's rumbling so loudly I'm sure the director's going to hear it and give me a dressing down, too.'

'You wouldn't want to get on the wrong side of Heston Gray,' a voice behind them said, and they spun around to see the woman in the wheelchair on the other side of the wall. 'He claims it's his artistic temperament, but in reality, he's nothing more than a bully.'

'You know him?' Poppy asked.

'Our paths have crossed a few times. I'm Krystal King, the horse master.'

Scarlett screwed up her face. 'Horse *master*?'

'That's what horse trainers are called on set. See Red Productions use my horses for all their period dramas.'

'Does the boy he shouted at work for you?'

'Ned?' She nodded. 'He's not the sharpest tool in the box, but I put up with him because he's good with the horses.'

'I'd much rather be a brilliant rider than an OK actor,' Poppy said.

'Quite right,' Krystal agreed, and Poppy flushed with pleasure.

Scarlett glanced over her shoulder. 'We should make ourselves scarce. They're about to start filming.'

'I'll come with you,' Krystal said. 'I need to make sure Perry's ready. He's in the scene they're shooting this afternoon.'

She pressed a button on the arm of her wheelchair, and it glided forwards.

'Is that the pony playing Merrylegs?' Scarlett asked. 'We saw him earlier.'

Krystal raised an eyebrow. 'The stables are supposed to be out of bounds for the crew and cast. Weren't you told?'

'Our friend Georgia owns Claydon Manor,' Poppy

explained. 'She was showing us around. I'm sorry. We didn't realise it wasn't allowed.'

'People have a habit of feeding the horses titbits, which sends them the wrong message. I use treats for training, not for standing in the stable looking pretty.'

Poppy's face reddened as she remembered the Polos she'd given Brian and Perry. 'They are all such beautiful horses,' she gabbled. 'Especially Isadore and Perry. In fact, Perry is the double of my pony, Cloud.'

The wheelchair came to a halt. 'He is?'

'Totally,' Scarlett said. 'Show Krystal a photo, Poppy.'

Poppy reached into the folds of her skirt for her phone and scrolled through the pictures until she found one of Cloud she'd taken after she'd bathed him the previous summer. For once, his dappled grey coat shone.

Krystal studied the photo. 'A Connie, is he? Fourteen two?'

Poppy nodded.

'I don't suppose he's for sale?'

7

Poppy wasn't sure she'd heard Krystal correctly. She pulled on an earlobe and stared at her.

'Pardon?'

'It's always good to have doubles in case you need a matching pair or a stand-in. Otherwise, the continuity girls get their knickers in a twist.'

'He's not for sale, no.'

'I pay well for the right horses.'

'It's not the money.'

Krystal looked her up and down. 'You'll be growing out of ponies soon and moving onto horses. You could buy something special.'

'Cloud is special. I don't want to sell him. Ever.'

Poppy lifted her chin and held Krystal's gaze. The older woman lowered her eyes first. 'Fair enough. But if you ever change your mind...'

'I won't,' Poppy said.

They reached the catering truck, and Scarlett's eyes widened at the array of dishes. Couscous salads and platters of cold meats and cheeses were arranged alongside a variety of quiches and baskets of rustic bread.

'This is way better than school dinners,' she said, grabbing a plate. 'I guess we help ourselves?'

'It's supposed to be cast and crew first, then extras,' Krystal said. 'But as both the cast and crew are otherwise engaged, I would say it's OK to fill your boots.'

Poppy handed Krystal a plate to show there were no hard feelings, and once she'd filled her plate, she joined Scarlett and Krystal at an empty table.

'Do you both ride?' Krystal asked.

They nodded.

'You might be interested in one of the stunt riding experience days I hold at my yard in Hampshire.'

'That sounds cool,' Scarlett said.

'They're very popular. I teach people trick riding skills, like how to sit on a rearing horse and how to lay a horse down. You learn how to carry weapons like swords or lances, and we finish the day with a bit of jousting.'

'My little brother would love it. He wants to be a stuntman if he can't get a job as a wildlife cameraman,' Poppy said.

'How much is it?' Scarlett asked.

'Two hundred pounds for the day, lunch included.'

Noticing Scarlett's shoulders droop, Poppy said, 'It sounds amazing, but it's a bit beyond our budget, unfortunately. We'll just have to teach our own ponies a few tricks, won't we, Scarlett? Cloud's old owner taught him to give her a kiss for a pony nut.'

Krystal buttered a roll. 'He's a quick learner, is he?'

'He seems to know what I want him to do before I even ask.'

'Red, too,' Scarlett said. 'He's my pony. He's only five, but he does TREC and everything. He's really brave.'

'Then he would make a brilliant trick pony,' Krystal said.

Poppy leaned forwards, her elbows on the table. 'It must be hard, training horses when you're in a wheelchair.'

'Did you have an accident?' Scarlett asked.

Krystal replaced her knife on her plate and popped the last piece of bread into her mouth. 'I broke my back when a young horse I was schooling over cross country fences had a rotational fall.'

Seeing their puzzled expressions, she said, 'It's when a horse hits a fence with his front legs or chest and somersaults over the fence. He landed on me when he fell. He wandered off with hardly a scratch on him, and I was left in this,' she gestured to her chair.

'But you still work with horses,' Poppy said. 'That's so brave.'

Krystal shrugged. 'Every cloud has a silver lining. Before my accident, I was indistinguishable from all the other horse trainers. Being in a wheelchair set me apart. Now everyone knows who I am. I have the best-trained horses in Europe. Producers are falling over themselves to employ me.'

'What would be the easiest trick to teach our ponies?' Scarlett asked.

As Krystal began explaining how she could teach Red to paw on command, Poppy noticed the runner they'd spoken to earlier sprinting from the house towards the catering truck.

He skidded to a stop by their table. 'Miss King?'

Krystal shrugged an apology to Scarlett and turned to him. 'What is it?'

'One of your horses, miss. It's making a terrible racket, banging and thrashing in its stable. I thought you should know.'

Krystal had already released the brake on her wheelchair. 'Fetch Ned and tell him to meet me at the stables,' she told the runner.

He blanched. 'What if they're still filming?'

'What's more important, the safety of my horse or a tinpot television show?' She eyed him dispassionately. 'Just do as I say.'

'We can help,' Scarlett said, springing up from her chair.

Krystal scowled at her legs. 'It's times like these I wish I hadn't…' She looked at the two girls. 'Can one of you run over to the stables?'

'I'll go,' Poppy said. Scarlett was faster over short distances, but Poppy was the best 800-metre runner in her year. Gathering the folds of her skirt in one hand, she raced towards the stables.

As Poppy drew near, she heard banging and crashing followed by a pitiful whinny. The sound sparked a memory of a snowy Boxing Day night years before. Weak with the flu, she'd found Cloud in his stable, drenched in sweat and grunting. When he'd sunk to his knees and started rolling wildly she'd known instinctively he had colic.

Somehow, they'd made it through the night, but it had been touch and go. *Please don't let this be colic*, she thought as she pounded across the spotless yard towards Perry's stable.

Almost too terrified to look, she steeled herself and gazed inside. The pony was lying on his side close to the back wall, his legs bent at an unnatural angle. Like Cloud he, too, was drenched in sweat and the whites of his eyes were showing. Sensing her presence, he struggled to stand, his legs flailing against the wooden kickboards.

'Hey, steady boy,' Poppy said in the calmest voice she could muster. Perry cocked an ear in her direction and fell still. Poppy slid the bolt across and slipped into the stable. Holding her hand out and keeping her eyes lowered, she inched forwards. Perry tried to stand again, but again his legs struck the wall uselessly. Poppy knelt down beside his head and stroked his cheek.

'I'm going to get your mum. She'll know what to do. You stay calm, OK? I'll be as quick as I can.'

As she raced back to Krystal and Scarlett, the banging started again, then stopped. Poppy wasn't sure which was worse, the clattering or the silence. Quickening her pace, she was soon running at full pelt, hoping with all her heart that Perry was going to be all right.

CAREERING around the corner of the indoor school, she almost ran slap bang into Krystal and Scarlett.

'He's on the floor, kicking at the wall,' she panted. 'He can't seem to get up.'

'Colic?' Krystal asked.

'I… I don't think so.'

The horse master nodded and fiddled with the controls on her wheelchair, increasing the speed until Poppy and Scarlett had to jog to keep up. Reaching Perry's stable, Krystal said, 'Can one of you open the door?'

Darting forwards, Poppy eased the door open. Perry was where she'd left him, lying parallel to the back wall. He made a half-hearted attempt to stand, then sank back on the straw bed as if all the life force had drained out of him.

'He's cast,' Krystal said. 'We need to get him back on his feet as soon as possible. Can you find two lead ropes?' she asked Scarlett.

She nodded and ran off towards Claydon's enormous tack room.

Poppy unbuttoned her jacket and threw it over the stable door. 'I've heard of it, but I don't really know what it means,' she admitted.

'It's when horses get stuck on their backs or sides and can't get back up because their legs are jammed against a wall or fence,' Krystal said. 'They need to have room to stretch their legs out to stand up. It's why you bank bedding up around the walls of a loose box. But even that doesn't stop some horses getting stuck.'

'Are you saying Perry literally can't stand up, even though he wants to?'

'Correct. And the longer a horse is down, the greater the risk of nerve damage and crush injuries. Some horses even die if they're not found soon enough.'

Poppy swallowed. 'Will Perry be OK?'

Krystal swept a weary hand across her face. 'I hope so.'

8

They waited in silence for Scarlett to return. Perry was trembling, his ears flicking back and forth. When Poppy crept across the stable to comfort him, he flinched and struck out with his near foreleg with such force that the wooden kick-board splintered.

'Be careful!' Krystal barked, and Poppy shrank back.

'Sorry.'

'Never, ever get between a horse and the wall it's cast against. You'll end up getting kicked, no matter how docile the horse normally is. Where's Scarlett with those lead ropes?'

'Here,' said a voice from outside. 'I picked the longest ones I could find.'

'Good.' Krystal gripped the arms of her wheelchair as if she was about to stand up, then slumped back, breathing out with a soft hiss like a deflating balloon.

Poppy stepped forwards. 'What do you need us to do?'

'Take a lead rope each, and loop it around Perry's offside legs just below the fetlock. Poppy, you take his foreleg, and Scarlett his hindleg. And be careful. He could kick out again at any moment.'

The two girls did as they were told, feeding the lead ropes around the gelding's legs.

'Now take his weight in your hands and pull very gently. All you're trying to do at this stage is drag him away from the wall so he can stand up himself.'

But the feel of the ropes tightening around his pasterns sent the gelding into a blind panic. He whinnied again, the high-pitched sound echoing around the four walls of the stable. His legs windmilled. Scarlett darted out of the way in time, but Poppy caught a glancing blow to her shin.

'Perry,' Krystal said, her voice low and urgent. 'Play dead!'

At once, the horse was still.

'Try again,' Krystal instructed.

The two girls took up the slack, dug their heels into the thick straw bed and heaved with all their might. It was like a desperate game of tug-of-war. But losing wasn't an option. Poppy's shoulders screamed in protest as she locked her arms and pulled. At first, it seemed as though they would never be able to move the grey gelding, but then, centimetre by centimetre, he began to slide away from the wall.

'Keep going,' Krystal said. 'You're nearly there.'

'Come on, Poppy. We've got this,' Scarlett said. 'On the count of three.'

'One… two… *three!*' they cried, hauling on the lead ropes. And Scarlett whooped as Perry slid towards them.

'Should we untie his legs?' Poppy said.

'No, we may need to roll him all the way over if he still can't stand up himself. But I think he'll be fine.'

Poppy and Scarlett exchanged a look. Perry hadn't so much as twitched a muscle in the last few minutes.

'Is he all right?' Scarlett asked in a quivery voice.

'Touch his shoulder and tell him to wake up,' Krystal said.

Poppy crouched down and touched the gelding's sweat-stained shoulder. 'Wake up Perry.'

At once, the pony opened his eyes, gave a little shake of his head, moved his legs experimentally, and rolled onto his belly. The lead ropes fell away as he unfolded his legs and pulled himself shakily to his feet.

'Thank goodness he's OK,' Scarlett said, beaming.

But Krystal was staring at Perry's near foreleg. She clicked her tongue and said, 'Perry, come,' and the pony walked alongside her wheelchair. She bent down and ran a hand along his cannon bone. He pinned his ears back and bared his teeth. 'Don't even think about it,' she told him. He retreated to the far corner of the stable.

Poppy could see immediately that something was wrong. 'He's hobbling.'

'Near fore,' Krystal agreed. 'His headcollar's hanging up outside the stable. Can you pass it to me?'

Poppy grabbed the leather headcollar and gave it to Krystal, who clicked her tongue again. Perry stumbled over, his head nodding with every step. Krystal slipped the headcollar on him and handed the lead rope to Scarlett.

'Can you trot him up outside?'

Poppy and Krystal watched as Scarlett led the gelding to the end of the yard and trotted him back towards them.

At a walk, his gait was unbalanced. But at a trot, he could barely place his weight on his near foreleg.

'What's he done?' Poppy asked.

'Strained a tendon, I should think,' Krystal said, her voice flat.

'Oh no! But that means weeks of box rest, doesn't it?'

'At least a month.'

'What about the filming? Will they wait for him to get better?'

'Nothing stops filming.' Krystal's hands were clenched around the arms of the wheelchair. 'I'll have to dose him up to his eyeballs with pain blockers and anti-inflammatories and hope he doesn't do himself any more damage.'

Poppy gaped. 'But that's...'

'Barbaric? I know. But production companies don't take no for an answer. I've signed a contract promising them the horses they need, and I need to fulfil that contract. Otherwise, they'll sue the pants off me.' Krystal paused. 'Of course, there is another way.'

'Then do it.'

'I'll need your help with that.'

'I don't understand.'

Krystal met her gaze. 'You said your pony was Perry's double. Lend him to me.'

9

P oppy wasn't sure she'd heard Krystal correctly. She shook her head and frowned. 'What?'

'Let me use your pony. I'll pay you.' The horse master named a figure that made Poppy's head spin.

'But Cloud isn't a stunt horse, he's just a regular pony.'

'You said his old owner taught him tricks. He's obviously quick to learn. And my training methods are the best in the world. I get results, fast.' Krystal said this matter-of-factly, without a trace of pride in her voice.

'But he's never been away from home before.' Not quite true, but Krystal didn't need to know he'd roamed free on Dartmoor for years.

'So many buts. Are you always this cautious? Think what an amazing experience it would be for him. He'd be one of the stars of a prime-time television show. Millions of people will fall in love with him. Think of the opportunities it will open up for you both. Magazines will be knocking on your door asking for interviews. Companies will be begging you to wear their brands. He may even get more television work off the back of it.'

'But he's not absolutely identical,' Poppy remembered with relief. 'So he isn't really Perry's double.'

'What do you mean?'

'Cloud has a grey muzzle, remember? Perry's is pink.'

Krystal waved a hand as if brushing away Poppy's concerns. 'Not a problem. The make-up girls can fix that. Do we have a deal?'

Scarlett coaxed a limping Perry back. His head nodded with every step and his tendon had already puffed up. There was no way he could continue filming. It was out of the question. But where would that leave Krystal? With her contract in tatters and an obligation there was no way she could meet.

Perhaps sensing she needed some space to think, Krystal took Perry from Scarlett, tied him up outside the stable and began hosing down his swollen tendon, humming to herself as she did. Poppy felt a little in awe of her. She was forthright and brusque, but a lot of horsey people were. Look at her friend Jodie Morgan, who ran Nethercote Horse Rescue. Jodie could be curt to the point of rudeness but her heart was in the right place and there was no questioning her love for her motley herd of rescue horses.

Scarlett brushed the white hairs off her black dress and joined Poppy. 'What's up? You've got that faraway look in your eye that usually spells trouble.'

Checking Krystal was still busy with Perry, Poppy motioned Scarlett to follow her into the tack room.

'It's Krystal. She wants Cloud to step in as Merrylegs.'

'Wow, really? But he's not a stunt horse.'

'That's what I said. Only she said she would train him. She'll also pay me.' Poppy repeated the figure Krystal had mentioned and Scarlett whistled.

'Crikey. She could have Red, Blaze *and* Flynn for that.'

'You'd let her have him, if you were me?'

'You bet I would. People pay a fortune to have their horses trained by someone like Krystal, and here she is, offering to pay you a seriously ridiculous amount of money to train him for you.'

Poppy bit her lip. 'I suppose. But it's all a bit sudden, isn't it? We've only just met her.'

'She's super cool though, isn't she? And while I was walking Perry I googled her. She's the country's leading stunt horse trainer.'

'You're saying I'd be mad not to?'

'You do tend to be over-cautious,' Scarlett said.

Poppy remembered her promise to throw caution to the wind and embrace new opportunities. She wanted to be less Poppy, more Scarlett, didn't she? And Scarlett would bite Krystal's hand off.

'OK,' she said, a smile creeping across her face. 'I'll tell her yes.'

But before she had a chance, the runner appeared, a clipboard in his hand and a harassed expression on his face.

'There you are! They're about to start filming your scene. You two need to get over to the main house ASAP.'

'I just need to tell Krystal something,' Poppy said, hopping from foot to foot.

'There's no time!'

Poppy cast one look back at Krystal. Scarlett tugged her sleeve.

'Come on, Poppy. We can't miss our moment of fame. You'll have to tell Krystal later.'

GEORGIA TAPPED her watch as Poppy and Scarlett arrived on set a few minutes later. Two make-up girls rushed over and brushed and re-tied their hair and dusted so much powder onto their faces that Poppy had to hold her nose to prevent a sneezing fit. One of the girls sighed as she flicked a wisp of hay from Poppy's collar.

Kelvin beckoned the extras over.

'In this scene Miss Flora and Miss Jessie are arriving home from school in the pony and trap.' The assistant director looked around. 'Where *is* the pony and trap?'

The runner sidled over, rubbing the back of his neck. 'Um, I'm afraid there's an issue with Merrylegs. Seems his legs are not so merry at the moment.' He gave a quick bark of laughter, then cleared his throat. 'What I mean to say is, he's hopping lame and he won't be going anywhere today.'

'That's what Krystal said?'

'Her exact words,' the runner confirmed.

The colour drained from Kelvin's face. 'Heston'll blow a fuse if filming's delayed. We're already way behind schedule.'

'Krystal told me to tell you not to worry because she has a Plan B. She said she'll be ready to shoot the scene on Monday.'

———

'So we haven't actually been in any scenes yet,' Poppy told her family as they sat around the kitchen table over dinner that evening.

'You're glad you signed up for it though?' her dad said.

'There's a lot of hanging around, but it's cool watching the horse scenes being filmed.' She speared a piece of sausage with her fork. 'Actually, I've got something to tell you.'

'Let me guess, they said you had a good face for radio.' Charlie sniggered.

'Hilarious,' Poppy said, rolling her eyes. 'The pony playing Merrylegs has strained a tendon and is on box rest. You won't believe it, but he looks like Cloud's identical twin. And guess what?'

'What?' Charlie said, his fork halfway to his mouth.

'The horse master has asked if she can hire Cloud to take his place, and I've said yes.'

Caroline and her dad exchanged a glance and Charlie's mouth fell open.

'But you hate anyone else riding Cloud, even Scarlett,' Charlie said.

'I used to when I was younger,' Poppy corrected him. 'And anyway, this isn't about me, it's about Cloud. This is a once-in-a-lifetime opportunity for him. And she's paying me a fortune.'

Charlie's eyebrows shot up. 'How much?'

'Enough to keep you in Lego for about two years.'

'What exactly is involved?' Caroline asked.

Poppy placed her knife and fork on her plate. 'Krystal - she's the horse master - will come over in the morning to pick Cloud up. He'll stay at Claydon Manor for the next two weeks while they finish filming the Birtwick Park scenes. Hopefully the pony playing Merrylegs will be sound by then.'

'And if he isn't?' her dad said. 'What happens then?'

Poppy blew her fringe out of her eyes. She'd assumed her family would be impressed by her news. Instead they seemed... wary. 'I don't know, it's probably in the contract.'

'You've signed a contract?' Caroline's voice was sharp.

'Of course. Everything needs to be legal and above board,' Poppy said primly. That's the phrase Krystal had used when she'd waved the contract under Poppy's nose as she and Scarlett had checked on Perry on their way home.

'Don't worry about reading the small print,' Krystal had said, producing a pen. 'It's a standard contract. No hidden nasties.'

Poppy had felt very grown up as she'd signed her name with a flourish.

'Where is it?' her dad asked.

'She's emailing it to me.' Poppy scowled at her family. 'You don't seem very excited.'

Caroline pushed her chair back and began clearing the table. 'Sorry, sweetheart. You're usually so protective of Cloud, that's all. It's taken us by surprise.' She squeezed Poppy's shoulder. 'But you're right, it's a wonderful opportunity for him and I'm sure everything will be absolutely fine.'

10

Poppy pulled on her wellies and stalked out of the back door and across the yard to Cloud's stable. She whistled and his familiar grey head appeared over the stable door. Offering him a Polo, she ruffled his forelock and let herself in, collapsing on the straw by his haynet.

All the excitement she'd felt about Cloud taking Perry's place had fizzled away after her family's luke-warm reception to the news. Instead an anxious little knot had formed in the pit of her stomach. Was she doing the right thing?

Cloud lowered his head and nudged her, in search of another treat. Once again, she was hit by the uncanny likeness between him and Perry. Did everyone have a double, somewhere in the world?

Poppy took a deep breath. 'I met a pony called Perry today who looks almost exactly like you,' she told him. 'At first I thought it was you, and I couldn't work out why you wouldn't come and say hello.'

Her voice caught, and she rubbed her face. 'The thing is, Perry's lame and he can't be in Black Beauty any more. I've said you'll take his place. A really cool horse trainer called Krystal is going to teach you loads of awesome new tricks. And she's going to pay us a whole heap of money that I can spend on things for you. Like that new rug I showed you? And the navy travel bandages. And some new leather boots for me. I can even buy Scarlett a new LeMieux saddle pad for the school showjumping team. And a matching fly veil if she wants one which, knowing Scarlett, she will.'

Poppy smiled as Cloud breathed warm, hay-scented air into her neck. 'Krystal's bringing her lorry over in the morning to pick you up. You're only going to Claydon Manor. It's where Georgia and Barley live, remember? So you won't be far from home. And I'll cycle over every day to see you.'

Cloud turned his back on Poppy and began pulling wisps of hay from his haynet. Was he cross with her, or simply hungry?

'You'd like to be on television, wouldn't you?' she said to his rump. 'Who doesn't want to be famous?'

It was a rhetorical question, which was just as well, because Cloud, busy with his haynet, had no answer. Not for the first time Poppy wished she knew what he was thinking. Because you could read all the books on horse psychology you liked, but the fact was you couldn't climb inside their heads to see the world from their eyes.

Somewhere outside an owl hooted and Poppy pulled herself to her feet.

'I suppose I'd better see if Caroline needs a hand with the washing up.' She leaned against her pony, her hand snaking around his neck to his chest. She could feel his heart beating in time with her own.

They were in sync. They always had been, always would be. Of course Poppy knew what was best for Cloud. He may have been as nervous as an unbroken colt when he'd first come off the moor, but these days he adored attention. He would love all the fuss and fanfare, of course he would.

BUT WHEN HER alarm went off at seven the following morning, the enormity of what she'd agreed to hit Poppy with the force of a hammer blow. She hadn't spent a night away from Cloud since she and Scarlett had spent a week pony trekking in the Forest of Dean.

'I'm going to feel as though I've lost a limb,' she admitted to Caroline over breakfast.

Her stepmum's eyebrows knotted. 'I'm sure it's not too late to change your mind if you're having second thoughts.'

'I've made a promise, Mum. I can't back out now. Anyway, I'll be fine. He's only down the road. I can pop over and see him whenever I want.'

'What time is this Krystal woman coming to pick him up?'

'Nine. She said she needs to spend the weekend training him before filming starts again on Monday.'

'Why don't you put your bike in the back of the lorry? You can settle Cloud in, then cycle home.'

'That's a brilliant idea. I will.' Poppy hugged her stepmum then stacked her plate in the dishwasher. 'I guess I'd better go and give him a quick bath so he's looking his best.'

When Poppy heard the rumble of a horse lorry an hour later, Cloud was gleaming and everything he could possibly need was packed in two plastic storage boxes.

Poppy dashed around to the front of the house to see Krystal's stuntrider, Ned, jumping down from the cab. He sauntered up to her and said, 'You have a horse for me?'

'Where's Krystal?' Poppy said, peering through the windscreen.

'She's back at the yard waiting for the vet.'

'How is Perry?'

'Standing on three legs. Reckon he's going to be off for months.' Ned let down the back ramp and swung open the last two partitions. 'Are you going to get this horse then?'

Poppy gave a quick nod. 'Won't be a sec.' She darted around to the stables and clipped Cloud's lead rope onto his headcollar.

'Time to go,' she said, leading him past the donkeys' stable. 'Say goodbye to Chester and Jenny.'

Jenny's seal-grey nose appeared over the door and she and Cloud nuzzled each other.

'Chester,' Poppy called. 'Come and say goodbye to Cloud.'

But the old donkey, standing in the shadows at the back of the stable, didn't move. Instead he fixed his chocolate brown eyes on Poppy and emitted a sorrowful hee-haw.

Cloud, picking up on his melancholy, whinnied back, and when Poppy turned to go, he planted all four feet on the ground and refused to budge.

'Ignore Chester. He's just sulking because he can't be on television with you.' Poppy tugged Cloud's lead rope. 'Come on, Ned's waiting.'

When Cloud still didn't move, Poppy flicked the lead rope against his flank and bellowed, 'Walk *on*.' Taken by surprise, his ears flicked back and he shot forwards. 'Pesky animals,' Poppy growled, as the lead rope burned her fingers.

'You can't blame them for acting up. They've hardly ever been apart,' Caroline said, appearing from the house with Charlie at her heels.

'Anyone would think Cloud's emigrating to flippin' New Zealand and we're never going to see him again,' Poppy muttered.

'You're right.' Caroline gave a brief smile and motioned to Poppy's bike, which was leaning against the tack room wall. 'Want me to wheel this round? I'd quite like to meet this Krystal woman.'

'Why do you insist on calling her "this Krystal woman"? Her name's Krystal. And anyway, she's not here. She's sent her stunt rider, Ned.'

'Stunt rider?' Charlie's jaw fell. 'D'you think he'll have time to show me a few tricks?'

'Absolutely not.'

'That's a nuisance. As your dad's in London for the next couple of weeks he asked me to run through the contract with her,' Caroline said. 'Seeing as she hasn't given you a copy.'

'She's going to email it to me. I told you that yesterday. And I expect she didn't come because it's difficult for her to get in and out of the cab. Seeing as she's in a wheelchair,' Poppy added pointedly.

Caroline winced. 'Of course, how thoughtless of me.'

Ned was lounging against the side of the lorry, scrolling through his phone. When he saw them, he did a double take.

'I see what you mean. He could be Perry's doppelganger.'

'His what?' Charlie said.

'Doppelganger. It means his lookalike,' Caroline told him. 'It's a German word which literally means doublewalker. They're often seen as the harbingers of doom.'

'Doomed, doomed, we're all *doomed*,' Charlie chanted. Poppy shook her head in despair.

Ned took the end of Cloud's lead rope and led him towards the back of the horsebox. But before he'd put a foot on the ramp the Connemara stopped, looked around and whinnied.

Somewhere behind the house a hee-haw rang back.

Ned pulled on the rope but Cloud refused to move.

'He's normally very good at loading,' Poppy said. 'Shall I try?'

Ned shrugged and handed her the lead rope.

Charlie capered towards her. 'Doomed, doomed, we're all...'

'Shut *up*!' she hissed, giving him a shove.

'Poppy!' Caroline chided.

'But he's always so *annoying*!' Poppy took a deep breath. She needed to stay calm if they were going to load Cloud. She scratched his poll and whispered in his ear. 'It's all right, baby. I'm coming with you.' She circled him so they could approach the ramp in a straight line. Without giving him a chance to hesitate, she clicked her tongue and marched up the ramp. 'Good boy,' she said, giving him a pat and tying him up.

Ned bolted the partition into place.

'I'll just grab my bike,' Poppy said.

'What does Krystal want with a bike?'

'It's for me, so I can cycle home once I've settled Cloud in.'

He frowned. 'Krystal didn't say anything about fetching you, too.'

Caroline, noticing the colour drain from Poppy's face, said, 'Why don't you give her a ring? I can't imagine she'd mind.'

'You don't know Krystal,' he muttered. Clamping his phone to his ear, he stepped away while Poppy, Caroline and Charlie stood awkwardly and tried to pretend they weren't listening to the one-sided conversation.

'It's Ned... Yeah, he's boxed but the girl wants to come with him. That's what I thought you'd say... Yeah, I know... OK, I'll tell her... Yep, see you later.'

He ambled over. 'Like I thought, owners aren't allowed to accompany their horses to the production sets. Krystal's training methods rely on the one-to-one bond she builds with the horses, and owners are a distraction. It was all in the contract you signed.'

'I can't even visit him on set?' Poppy cried.

Ned gave another laconic shrug. ''Fraid not, no.'

He jumped back in the cab, switched on the ignition and threw the gearstick into reverse.

'But you can't…' Poppy cried, running towards the driver's door. Caroline grabbed her arm and pulled her back.

'Don't worry, sweetheart. I'm sure it's all a silly misunderstanding. I'll sort it out.'

As they watched the lorry disappear down the Riverdale drive Poppy told herself Caroline was right. Krystal had said Ned wasn't the sharpest tool in the box. He must have got the wrong end of the stick, that was all. There was nothing to worry about. She'd be able to visit Cloud as often as she liked.

11

Monday morning arrived, and Poppy was awake with the dawn, itching to return to Claydon Manor to see Cloud.

Caroline had tried calling the contact number on Krystal's website countless times over the weekend, but it went straight to voicemail every time. After leaving half a dozen messages asking her to call, Caroline had given up.

Poppy had wandered around the stables and paddocks feeling discombobulated. Everything felt out of kilter. Lop-sided. As if she'd lost an arm or a leg. Grateful she still had Chester and Jenny to look after, she'd kept herself busy, attacking the nettles that had already begun their annual invasion of the muckheap, reorganising the tack room and using the opportunity to give Cloud's empty stable a deep clean.

Chester wasn't himself, either. 'He's eating OK, but he keeps looking out over the moor and calling to Cloud,' Poppy had told Caroline.

'It's only to be expected. They've hardly ever been apart.' Caroline had given Poppy's shoulder a squeeze. 'Think how pleased he'll be when they're reunited.'

Eventually, Poppy had swallowed her pride and texted Georgia.

Just wondered how Cloud is settling in. Have you seen any of his training sessions?

A reply pinged back a few minutes later.

I've seen him from a distance and he seems fine. But Krystal's taken over the indoor school for training and no-one's allowed anywhere near. Surprised you haven't been over to see him.

Poppy bit her lip.

I would have, only I'm not allowed. Apparently I'd be a 'distraction'.

Blimey, Krystal's more of a diva than me! Georgia had typed back, adding a couple of laughing emojis. *Don't you worry, I'll keep an eye on him for you.*

———

POPPY WHEELED her bike down to the end of the drive where she'd arranged to meet Scarlett so they could cycle over to Claydon Manor for the day's filming.

While she waited, she pulled up handfuls of grass and fed them to three lambs who gambolled over to the gate to see her. Having been bottle-fed since birth by Scarlett's mum, they were so tame they let her stroke their heads and tickle their chins.

The lambs heard Scarlett's singing before Poppy did and they careened across the field, as skittish as kittens.

'You terrified the lambs with your caterwauling,' Poppy said as Scarlett executed a pretty impressive skid stop beside her.

'There's no accounting for taste.' Scarlett held her nose in the air and gave an exaggerated sniff, then burst out laughing.

'You're in a good mood this morning,' Poppy remarked.

'You would be too if your parents had just given you the latest iPhone and it wasn't even your birthday or Christmas or anything.'

Poppy's jaw dropped. 'Wow.'

'I know. It still hasn't sunk in. Look how cool it is.' Scarlett waved the phone in Poppy's face. 'It has a triple-lens camera, facial recognition and toughened glass that hopefully even I won't be able to break. Oh, and more than five hundred gigabytes of storage so I'll have plenty of space to record all my films for Instagram.'

Poppy jumped on her bike and began pedalling down the lane. Scarlett zipped the phone back in her pocket and followed.

'It's really cool, Scar. But I thought things were tight on the farm?'

Scarlett's beaming smile slipped a little. 'They are. But Mum used her rainy day money. I didn't ask her to, but she knew how upset I was when I broke my screen. And that phone was a hand-me-down from Alex. She said it was about time I had something new, just for me.'

'You'll have to be super careful with it. No recording while you're galloping.'

'Don't worry, I will be,' Scarlett said, patting her pocket. 'Barney said they're shooting in the village today. Forge Lane, where all the old stone cottages are.'

Barney Broomfield, the owner of Waterby Post Office and Stores, kept his ear to the ground and broadcast the news days before it appeared in the Tavistock Herald.

'Barney says the production company has drafted in a load more extras for the scene.' Scarlett looked sidelong at Poppy. 'It's the one where Squire Gordon and Miss Flora ride Black Beauty and Merrylegs into the village to pin up a wanted poster for the highwaymen.'

Poppy's bike hit a pothole, and she almost flew straight over the handlebars.

'Apparently, the actress who's playing Miss Flora had to have a crash course in riding, and she's been practising on Cloud all weekend,' Scarlett continued.

'Bully for her,' Poppy grumbled as she righted herself in the saddle. 'How does Barney know, anyway?'

'The cast and crew have been in and out of the shop all week. Barney's been joking that he'd be able to take early retirement if the filming went on any longer. You should see the number of sweets they get through. I'm surprised they have any teeth left.'

Poppy couldn't care less about the state of the cast and crew's teeth. All she cared about was seeing Cloud again. Since Ned had driven away on Saturday morning, she hadn't been able to shift the pain in her chest.

It wasn't as needle-sharp as a stitch, more a weary ache that she could only assume was sorrow. Which was ridiculous, because while she was moping around at home, Cloud was probably having the time of his life.

They reached Claydon Manor and pedalled down the drive.

'It's still only a quarter to nine. I'm going to say hello to Cloud before filming starts,' Poppy said, leaning her bike against the wall of the house.

'I thought you said you weren't supposed to,' Scarlett began.

Poppy shrugged. 'I won't tell if you don't.'

There was a spring in her step as she headed towards the yard, her hand closing around the carrot she'd pinched from the vegetable rack before she'd left home. As she walked along the row of loose boxes, she glanced into each.

Brian, the heavyweight hunter playing Sir Oliver, was too busy demolishing his haynet to pay her any attention. Isadore's stable was empty bar a laden wheelbarrow and a fork. Roxie, the chestnut mare, whinnied when she saw Poppy. Poppy looked around nervously as she rubbed the mare's face and shushed her.

A length of hose was coiled like a snake outside Perry's loose box. Poppy peered over the door. The grey gelding was standing at the back of the box with his rump facing her. Curious to see just how lame he was, she snapped off the end of the carrot and whistled. But just as before, he ignored her. Poppy shrugged and left him to it. She was only interested in Cloud anyway.

Dozing in the next three loose boxes were the three bays who'd played the highwaymen's horses. Poppy quickened her pace to the last box in the row.

'Cloud,' she called. He whickered, and her heart skipped a beat as she fished the carrot out of her pocket. The urge to fling her arms around his neck and never let him go was overwhelming. But as he walked towards her Poppy stiffened. He couldn't put any weight on his near foreleg. Her eyes were drawn to the bright red bandage that encased his leg from his fetlock to his knee. It was the same leg Perry had injured. Poppy stared blankly at the neatly-wrapped bandage as her mind whirled. Had Cloud sprained a tendon, too? How and when had it happened? And, the biggest question of all, why hadn't Krystal told her?

He nuzzled her hand. She offered him the carrot on autopilot, her focus still on his leg. As his whiskers tickled her wrist, she stroked his head, her hand tracing a line from his poll to his nose. Her eyes fell on his pink muzzle, and she raised her eyebrows.

'Crikey, that's convincing,' she said. 'I wonder what they used.'

She licked her thumb, rubbed it against his muzzle and inspected it. Nothing. Not even a smudge of pink make-up. And that was when a trace of unease lodged itself in her chest.

Her eyes travelled over the pony, from his pink muzzle to the tips of his ears to his tail, which longer than Cloud's had been the day he'd left for Claydon Manor.

Poppy took a step backwards as the realisation hit

her. This wasn't Cloud, it was his double. Poor, lame Perry.

And if this was Perry, that could only mean one thing. The pony who'd rejected her overtures was Cloud.

efore Poppy had a chance to dart back to Cloud's stable, Scarlett pelted into the yard.

'Poppy, we need to go, like, literally now. Georgia said Kelvin's briefing the extras in about,' she checked her watch, 'thirty seconds.'

'But...' Poppy began, waving an arm in Cloud's direction.

'No time for buts. Come on,' Scarlett said, pulling Poppy towards the set.

The assistant director was already talking when they arrived, so they made their way to the back of the group, hoping no-one had noticed.

'... you're not being paid to talk. Don't say anything during a take, and don't talk between takes, either,' Kelvin was saying. Having heard it all before, Poppy's thoughts snapped back to Cloud. Not once in all the years she'd owned him had he given her the cold-shoulder. He was affectionate and loyal, always the first to whicker or give her a friendly nuzzle. When he'd come off the moor, she was the only person he'd trusted. Everyone commented on the strong bond they had. So why had he blanked her?

Poppy became aware that Scarlett was muttering under her breath and surreptitiously pointing to their right.

'What?' she said, loudly enough to earn her a disapproving look from the assistant director.

'George Blackstone,' Scarlett hissed.

Poppy stood on tiptoes and scanned the motley collection of extras. Sure enough, leaning on a shepherd's crook over to their right was a grey-haired man in a flat cap and a threadbare tweed jacket. The same man who'd beaten Cloud senseless and had sent him, half-starved and terrified, to the annual pony sales where Poppy's dad had bought him.

Even the sight of Blackstone was enough to make her skin crawl.

'What on earth is he doing here?' she whispered back.

'Probably here for the money,' Scarlett said. And, sure enough, when Kelvin finished his briefing and asked if anyone had any questions, the old hill farmer held up a grimy hand.

'When do we get paid?' he wheezed.

Kelvin looked askance. 'Peggy will take everyone's bank details, and the money will be transferred into your accounts at the end of the month.'

Another farmer with a weathered face standing beside Poppy gave a loud guffaw.

'Old Blackstone won't like that. He only deals in cash, don't you, George!'

George Blackstone muttered something under his breath and shot a filthy look at the farmer. His gaze fell on Poppy and Scarlett, and his eyes bulged. Poppy resisted the urge to turn tail and flee.

He's just a bully, she reminded herself. She'd stood up to him in the past, and she would do again without hesitation if she needed to.

Kelvin clapped his hands. 'Please change into your costumes and be on the coach for the drive to the village by half-past.'

POPPY LOOKED AROUND with interest as she jumped off the coach. Forge Lane was a picturesque cobbled street lined with pretty brick and flint houses with a pub, the Farriers Arms, at the far end. The cars that were usually parked either side of the road had gone, and See Red Productions had temporarily set up home in the pub car park.

Krystal's horse lorry was parked behind the catering van, and Poppy stood on tiptoes to see if she could catch a glimpse of Cloud. She dropped back on her heels and sighed.

'What's up?' said Scarlett, who was playing a village girl in the scene, swapping her maid's costume for a pencil-lead grey dress with a pinafore over the top.

'I can't see Cloud.'

'Did you say Cloud?' said a voice behind Poppy. She turned to see a girl around her age dressed in a fitted black jacket and flared-hip breeches the colour of butter. The girl held out a hand. 'I'm Heidi Holland. I play Miss Flora,' she added, registering Poppy's blank expression.

'Oh my God, I saw you in Dr Who. You were brilliant,' Scarlett said, whipping out her new phone. 'Mind if I take a selfie?'

'Not at all.' Heidi leaned in close to Scarlett and turned on a high wattage smile as Scarlett clicked away.

'Cool, thanks,' Scarlett said, inspecting the photo. 'I'll add it to my Instagram Stories if that's OK?'

'Of course!' Heidi turned her attention to Poppy. 'Are you Cloud's owner?'

'Um, yes.'

'He is just the *cutest!*' Heidi said, her hands waving expansively. 'He has the kindest eyes, and the most delicious whiskery kisses. I've spent virtually all weekend with him. I've discovered muscles in places I didn't even know muscles *existed!*' She grimaced, peeled with laughter, then looked over her shoulder to make sure no-one was in earshot. 'I may have exaggerated my riding ability just a *teeny-weeny* bit when I auditioned for the part. But Krystal's given me a crash course, and Cloud's been an absolute angel. He's so much easier to ride than Perry. You should be so proud of him.'

Poppy could only mumble, 'I am.'

'I love the way he goes all gooey when you scratch the bottom of his ear. And the way he really seems to know what you're saying when you talk to him. We just seemed to click the moment we met, you know?'

'Heidi!' Kelvin yelled from the pub car park. 'You're needed in make-up.'

Heidi shot them an apologetic smile. 'I'd better go. It was lovely to meet you both.'

'You, too. I'm Scarlett, by the way, and this is Poppy. We're here all week. Did you start out as an extra, too?'

Heidi flashed a set of perfect white teeth that clearly hadn't been anywhere near Barney's sweets. 'No, I go to the Italia Conti Academy of Theatre Arts in London.'

'Of course you do,' Poppy muttered.

Scarlett coughed loudly and said, 'How exciting. We'll see you around, yeah?'

'I'd *love* that! Between you and me, the girl playing Miss Jessie's a bit up herself. It would be cool to have someone to hang out with.' And she spun on her heels and strode off towards the car park.

'Crikey, what must Miss Jessie be like if Heidi Holland thinks she's up herself,' Poppy said.

'What d'you mean? She's lovely. Really approachable and friendly. You'd never know she was famous.'

'Famous?' Poppy snorted. 'Hardly. She had a walk-on role in Dr Who and has probably appeared in an episode of Doctors like a million other bit-part actors.'

Scarlett stared at Poppy slack-jawed. 'Wow, that was catty. What's Heidi done to rattle your cage?'

'What do you think? "We just seemed to click the moment we met",' Poppy mimicked. 'She doesn't even know Cloud. What a stupid thing to say.'

Scarlett's face cleared. 'And suddenly everything

makes sense. You're *jealous*. Silly me, I forgot how possessive you are of him. Shouldn't you be pleased that the person riding him is fond of him and will treat him well?'

Poppy rubbed her face. 'Don't be stupid, of course I'm pleased. And I'm not possessive. I just want the best for him. But she's so… gushing. And she's a liar.'

'What?'

'She lied about being able to ride to get the part. What else has she lied about?'

Scarlett fixed Poppy with a stern look. 'What's all this really about?'

Poppy went to plunge her hands in her pockets, only the stupid skirt had none, and she was left with her arms swinging uselessly by her sides. 'I saw Cloud in his stable this morning…' Her voice wobbled.

'That's good, isn't it?'

'No, you don't understand! He didn't want to know me. He didn't even come and say hello.' She sniffed. 'It was like I was… like I was *invisible*.'

In the distance, Kelvin was summoning the extras. Scarlett threaded her arm through Poppy's, and they made their way to the car park.

'Don't worry, he's probably sulking,' she said. 'Meg does it every time we stay at Granny's. He'll get over himself.'

'You think?'

'Definitely,' Scarlett said, patting Poppy's arm. 'You're the most important person in his life. Anyone can see that. You two have an amazing bond.'

'But Caitlyn had an amazing bond with him before she died. What if Cloud decides he has an amazing bond with Heidi, too? An even more amazing bond than with me? I couldn't bear it.'

'He'll forget all about her once he's home.'

'Maybe.' Poppy exhaled loudly. 'I wish I'd never agreed to all this,' she said, waving her hands at the set.

'Why did you?'

'Because I thought it would be great for Cloud. One

of those once-in-a-lifetime adventures that most people would give their eye teeth for. And you said I should do it.'

Scarlett dropped Poppy's arm. 'Don't blame me. Would you jump out of a window if I told you to? No, I didn't think so. Just chill a bit and enjoy the experience, for goodness' sake.' And she stomped off down the road towards the pub car park, her skirt swishing.

Stung, Poppy dawdled behind. Why had she let Krystal borrow Cloud? She'd been flattered to be asked, there was no question about that. And the money was not to be sniffed at, either. But an annoying little voice in her head told her it wasn't just the money or the flattery. *You wanted to bask in his reflected glory*, whispered the voice. *You wanted some of his fame to rub off on you.* Poppy McKeever, owner of television's favourite equine star, Cloud Nine.

There was a horse vlogger not much older than Poppy who had almost two hundred thousand followers on Instagram. More than three million people watched her YouTube channel every month. Her horse only had to sneeze to get thirty thousand likes. Poppy never missed her weekly videos on riding and horse care. She liked and commented on the vlogger's daily Instagram posts.

Sure, she was showered with the kind of free stuff Scarlett coveted, but that wasn't why Poppy secretly idolised her. It was the opportunities being a social media influencer had given her. She was an ambassador for international horse welfare charities. She got to meet the biggest names in showjumping, dressage and eventing. And she was a VIP guest at all the big equestrian events, from Hickstead to the Horse of the Year Show. Pony-mad kids queued for hours just to take a selfie with her.

Poppy didn't want to be recognised as she walked down the street. That kind of fame wasn't for her. But to have a high profile in the horsey world would be pretty cool.

And that, if she was totally honest, was why she'd agreed to let Krystal borrow Cloud.

THE EXTRAS GATHERED around Kelvin as he briefed them on their roles. The expressions on their faces ranged from expectant to plain bored.

'Schoolgirls,' he said, presenting Georgia with a length of rope. 'You're going to be skipping outside the pub.'

'Skipping?' Georgia echoed, holding out her skirt. 'In this? You've got to be kidding me.'

Ignoring her, Kelvin turned to George Blackstone and the chairman of the parish council. 'Peasants, you're perusing the village noticeboard when Squire Gordon and Miss Flora arrive on horseback. Squire Gordon will hand you -' he pointed to Blackstone, 'his reins while he pins up his wanted poster. When he's done you hand him back his reins and touch your cap. Got it?' They murmured assent.

'Village children, you're playing marbles in the dirt. The camera will be on you when the scene opens and will then pan across to the horses as they gallop in. Right, let's have a quick run-though before the actors arrive.'

Once Kelvin was happy they all knew what they were supposed to be doing, he disappeared. Poppy took the opportunity to apologise to Scarlett.

'Sorry I snapped. I know I'm over-reacting,' she said.

'It's all right. I'd probably be a bit jealous, too. But remember what Iago told Othello?'

They'd not long started studying the Shakespeare play in English. Poppy cast her mind back. 'Something about green eyes?'

'Exactly!' Scarlett said, touching her nose with one hand and pointing at Poppy with the other. '"O beware, my lord, of jealousy. It is the green-eyed monster which doth mock the meat it feeds on."'

'But what does that actually mean?'

Scarlett grinned. 'No idea. But it doesn't sound good, does it?'

Kelvin stepped back into their midst. 'Everyone to their stations, please.'

Poppy joined Georgia and Fiona on the cobbles outside the pub. The two older girls each picked up an end of the rope.

'Hey Georgia, I thought you were going to skip,' Poppy said in alarm.

'Changed my mind. You can do it,' Georgia said.

'But I haven't had a chance to practice. What if I mess up?'

'They'll have to do another take until you get it right.'

'Quiet on set!' Kelvin shouted. 'Roll sound!'

Poppy tried to ignore the butterflies in her stomach as the crew went through the motions. All she had to do was jump in time with the turn of the rope. She'd learned to skip when she was about six. It would be fine.

'Scene twenty-six, take one.' Kelvin slammed the clapperboard shut. 'And… action!'

Poppy was so focused on not tripping up or turning her ankles on the cobbles that when the clatter of hooves rang out in the pretty street, she kept her eyes glued on the skipping rope.

The actor playing Squire Gordon said, 'Take my reins, good fellow.' Cloud whinnied, his shrill call slicing through the air. Someone shrieked, and Kelvin yelled, 'Cut!'

The skipping rope fell slack as Georgia and Fiona gazed open-mouthed at the actors. With a feeling of dread, Poppy turned around. Cloud was backing up the cobbled street, his head high and his nostrils flared. Heidi Holland's arms were wrapped around his neck as she clung on for dear life.

Poppy's hand flew to her mouth. 'What happened?'

'He was fine until they reached the noticeboard,' Georgia said. 'Then he spooked at something and almost threw Miss Flora off.' For once, there wasn't even a trace of scorn in her voice.

Members of the crew tried to grab Cloud's reins as he

passed, but their shouts and waving arms only terrified him further. Poppy knew that at any moment he could spin around and flee, with or without Heidi on his back.

Without thinking, she lifted her skirts and ran up the hill as fast as her legs would carry her. When she was within a few metres of him, she slowed to a walk and called, 'Hey Cloud, it's me.'

His ears flickered forwards, and he hesitated.

'There's a good lad.' She took a step forwards, and another. Cloud came to a halt, and Poppy held out her hand for him to sniff. As he extended his neck towards her, she grabbed his reins.

'Are you all right?' she asked Heidi.

Wriggling back into the saddle, the young actor nodded. 'Thanks to you.'

Behind her, the whirr of an electric wheelchair grew louder, and Poppy turned to see Krystal bumping up the cobbles towards them, closely followed by a puce-faced Kelvin.

'What the heck was all that about? He was fine in the run-through.'

'I have no idea,' Krystal said, shaking her head.

But Poppy had worked it out. She could have kicked herself for not seeing the danger sooner. She'd been so preoccupied that it wasn't until she'd run past the two peasants standing by the noticeboard that everything had dropped into place.

Cloud was the bravest pony she knew. But there was one thing he was terrified of. Well, to be precise, one person.

George Blackstone.

14

'Y ou mean they sent George Blackstone home?' Scarlett said, her eyes wide.

'Only for the rest of the day. Kelvin was very understanding when I explained why Cloud had reacted so badly. He promised that they won't use Blackstone in any of the scenes with the horses in and they're going to reshoot this morning's scene later with a different peasant.'

'And what about Krystal?'

Poppy was silent. Krystal had been harder to read. She'd made sympathetic noises and had given Cloud a brisk pat, but her expression had seemed strained as she'd instructed Ned to lead him back to the horsebox.

Poppy, on the other hand, felt more cheerful than she had all morning. Once Heidi had scrambled out of the saddle and disappeared to have her make-up touched up and her hair restyled, she'd spent a whole ten minutes with Cloud. And, after she'd scratched his poll and ran soothing hands down his neck and generally made a big fuss of him, he appeared to have forgiven her.

The two girls wandered down to the catering lorry and helped themselves to a fruit juice.

'My followers are loving all the behind-the-scenes photos of the set,' Scarlett said, sipping her drink.

'"My followers?" You sound like a dodgy cult leader.' Scarlett giggled.

'How many d'you have now?'

'As of this morning, almost fifteen hundred.'

'Crikey. I'll take a picture of your new outfit if you like.'

'Thanks. I'll get my phone.' Scarlett tramped across to the coach that had brought them over from Claydon Manor. Poppy drank her juice and let her mind drift. She was halfway through an enjoyable little daydream in which she and Cloud were guests of honour at the Christmas Finale at Olympia when Scarlett sprinted to her side.

'I can't find my phone!'

'You left it in your rucksack, didn't you?'

Scarlett nodded. 'In the inside pocket. But it's not there now.'

Poppy set down her juice and pushed her chair back. 'Are you sure?'

Scarlett's voice rose. 'Of course I'm sure! It's gone, I'm telling you.'

'Show me.'

Poppy clambered onto the coach behind Scarlett and followed her along the aisle to their seats. The contents of Scarlett's rucksack had been upended on the blue and red patterned upholstery. Poppy's eyes travelled over her purse, lip salve, a well-thumbed copy of The One Dollar Horse, a packet of travel tissues, a hairbrush and a small bottle of water. There was no phone.

'Let me check your rucksack in case you've missed it,' she said, reaching for the bag and unzipping every pocket. Apart from some hair clips and a scrunchie, they were all empty.

'I told you,' Scarlett said, close to tears. 'Someone's stolen it.'

'I'm sure there must be another explanation.'

'Like what?'

'If it was stolen, why would the thief have left your purse?' Poppy said, picking up the oilcloth wallet with little white horses capering over it.

'Because there's nothing in it except receipts,' Scarlett said, tipping the wallet upside down to prove her point. She let out a wail. 'What am I going to tell Mum? She spent all her rainy day money on my phone.'

'Let me see if mine's still there,' Poppy said. She ferreted through her rucksack. Her mobile, a battered iPhone that her dad had given her when he'd bought a new one a couple of years ago, was there. So was her purse. But when Poppy checked to see if the twenty-pound note Tory had given her for her birthday was inside it she, too, cried out. 'They've stolen my birthday money!'

'Pass me your phone,' Scarlett instructed. 'I'm calling 999.'

'Don't you think we should tell someone on set

first? You can't have the police turning up halfway through a take. Let's find the casting director lady. Peggy, wasn't it? She seemed nice.'

'All right.' Scarlett frowned and pointed to a seat two rows in front of theirs. 'How did we miss this?'

Another rucksack had been emptied onto the seat.

'No phone or purse,' Poppy said, sifting through the contents. 'Seems we're not the only ones the thief picked on.'

'Isn't that where Georgia and Fiona were sitting?'

Poppy held up a plastic card. It was Georgia's bus pass. 'We'd better tell Peggy,' she said grimly.

They found Peggy in a huddle by the catering van with Kelvin and a couple of other members of the crew. Seeing them loitering, Peggy waved them over.

'Everything all right?'

'Not really,' Scarlett said. 'My new phone's been stolen from the coach.'

'And someone's taken some money from my purse,' Poppy said. 'We were going to call 999 but thought we ought to report it to you first.'

Peggy glanced at Kelvin, who frowned.

'How do you know they've been stolen? The coach is supposed to be locked during filming,' he said.

'Well, it wasn't,' Scarlett answered.

'The door was wide open,' Poppy agreed.

Peggy touched Kelvin's arm. 'I think it's time we called the police, don't you?'

Kelvin ran a hand through his hair and groaned. 'But we're already way behind schedule. Having PC

Plod and his friends turn up in force is not going to help.'

'But what about my phone? It's brand new,' Scarlett wailed.

'It's all right,' Peggy soothed as she led the girls to an empty table. 'I'm sure it'll turn up. Would you like a drink?'

They nodded and waited in silence as Peggy brought over two fresh glasses of juice.

'This isn't the first theft, is it?' Poppy said, watching the older woman's face closely.

Peggy sighed. 'A purse belonging to one of the camera operators went missing yesterday.'

'Why didn't you warn everyone?' Scarlett said.

'She wasn't one hundred per cent sure she hadn't mislaid it. But it looks as if it must have been stolen, too.'

'We saw another bag on the coach that had been ransacked,' Poppy said. 'Which makes at least four thefts.'

Peggy tutted. 'Nothing like this has ever happened before. We're like one big family.' She pushed her chair back. 'Now if you two girls are OK, I'll check how Kelvin's getting on with the police.'

'What kind of person helps themselves to other people's things?' Scarlett said once she'd gone.

'I can make a pretty educated guess, can't you?'

'What d'you mean?'

'Our thief has to be someone with no conscience who doesn't give a monkey's about anyone else.

Someone who is obsessed with money and wouldn't think twice about breaking the law to make a few quid.'

Scarlett clutched Poppy's hand. 'Are you saying it was George Blackstone?'

'It's got to be, hasn't it? He appears on set, and suddenly things start disappearing.'

'I suppose it makes sense.'

'We're talking about a man who stole a donkey, assisted in a kidnapping and ran an illegal puppy farm. Of course it's him. And that's exactly what I'm going to tell the police when they arrive.'

15

'What did your mum say when you told her about your phone?' Poppy asked Scarlett as they cycled to Claydon Manor the next morning.

Scarlett pulled a face. 'I haven't told her yet. I know how disappointed she'll be.'

'Hasn't she noticed you're not using it?'

'I've been using my old one. You know Mum, she's not exactly tech-savvy. A phone's a phone to her.'

'You're going to have to tell her at some point.'

Scarlett groaned. 'I'm hoping it'll turn up. Stupid, I know.'

Once again, Kelvin outlined the day's filming schedule and ran through the dos and don'ts. 'One last thing,' he said before the extras made their way to the costume lorry. 'You may see a couple of people in police uniform on set this morning. They are real police officers, not actors, so don't give them any cheek or you may end up being arrested.'

One of the extras tittered.

'They're here to investigate some thefts we've had in the last couple of days,' Kelvin said. 'Please co-operate if they want to speak to you. The sooner we catch the culprit, the better.'

'Hear, hear,' Poppy muttered, her gaze fixed on George Blackstone. His piggy eyes met hers for a brief moment before he spat in the dirt. It took all of Poppy's willpower not to react. Instead, she nudged Scarlett. 'C'mon, let's get changed.'

Scarlett was back in her scullery maid's uniform for the first scene, in which Squire and Mrs Gordon were arriving back at Birtwick Park after a carriage trip to London.

With Krystal and Ned busy on set with Isadore and Roxie, Poppy decided to seize the opportunity to spend half an hour with Cloud. Checking no-one was watching, she slipped between the production lorries, heading for the stables.

She was tiptoeing past the coach when someone cleared their throat, and she jumped out of her skin.

'Well, I never! If it isn't young Poppy McKeever,' boomed a voice.

Poppy spun around to see a man in a police uniform watching her, an amused expression on his face.

'Inspector P-Pearson,' she stuttered.

'Now there's a guilty face if ever I saw one,' the inspector said to someone out of Poppy's view. 'Skulking around up to no good, I dare say.' He chuckled, his multiple chins wobbling like jelly.

'Hunting for evidence, if I know Poppy. Trying to do us out of a job,' said a woman. Poppy could hear the smile in her voice, and her shoulders relaxed a little.

PC Claire Bodiam stepped out from behind the parked vehicles. When she saw Poppy's outfit, she smiled. 'There was no need to go to so much trouble for us.'

'I didn't. I mean, it's my costume. I'm a Victorian schoolgirl,' Poppy said, flustered.

'Why are you creeping around behind the scenes and not on set with all the other extras?' Inspector Pearson asked.

Poppy hesitated. Visits to the stables were banned. But only on Krystal's orders. It wasn't the law.

'I was going to see Cloud. My pony,' she added for the inspector's benefit.

'What's Cloud doing here?' PC Bodiam asked.

'He's starring as Merrylegs,' Poppy said, failing to hide the pride in her voice. 'He stepped in when the pony who was supposed to be playing him went lame.'

'How exciting,' PC Bodiam said. 'So we'll see him on our screens later this year?'

'That's the plan.' Poppy looked from one to the other. 'Are you here about the thefts?'

Inspector Pearson nodded. 'I wouldn't normally come myself, but it was a quiet morning back at the nick.'

'And he has a soft spot for the actress playing Mrs Gordon,' PC Bodiam added, winking at Poppy.

'She's in the scene they're filming at the moment,' Poppy said. 'Will you be interviewing everyone about the thefts? Only I had some money stolen, and my friend Scarlett's brand-new iPhone was nicked.'

'We'll be taking details from all the victims,' PC Bodiam confirmed. 'Why don't we find somewhere to sit?'

'Preferably near a tea urn and a packet of biscuits,' Inspector Pearson added.

'Now?' Poppy said, her eyes darting to the stables. Who knew how long she had before Krystal and Ned were back.

'It'll only take five minutes.'

'The catering truck's this way.' Poppy led the officers to the truck and fetched two cups of tea and a plate of rich tea biscuits while they settled themselves at a table. PC Bodiam pulled a notebook from her top pocket and thumbed through it until she found a new page.

'You had some money stolen, you say?' she said, as her inspector dipped a rich tea biscuit into his cup and popped it in his mouth, grunting with satisfaction.

'Twenty pounds,' Poppy confirmed. 'It was taken from my rucksack, which I'd left on the coach.'

'Time frame?'

Poppy thought back. 'It must have been between half nine and twelve while they were shooting a scene in Forge Lane.'

'Did you see anyone acting suspiciously in the area between those times?'

'Erm, no.'

'You don't seem very sure.'

'I didn't actually see anyone acting suspiciously, but I can tell you who the thief is.'

'You can?' Inspector Pearson said.

Poppy glanced over her shoulder to make sure no-one was in earshot. 'George Blackstone,' she said in an undertone.

'*Blackstone?*'

'He's an extra,' Poppy said. 'Playing a peasant. He was filming in Forge Lane yesterday, too. The driver left the coach unlocked. It would have been easy for Blackstone to slip inside and rifle through everyone's bags.'

PC Bodiam tapped the end of her pen against her chin. 'But you didn't actually see him do this?'

'No,' Poppy admitted. 'But it all makes sense, doesn't it? The man's a crook through and through. Of course it was him. Who else would it be?'

'Just because you don't like someone doesn't mean they're guilty. We need hard evidence,' Inspector Pearson said.

'I'll -' Poppy began.

PC Bodiam's hand shot out as if she was stopping traffic. 'Don't even think about it. You leave the police work to us. Rest assured we'll be interviewing everyone who was on set yesterday.'

'Including George Blackstone?'

'Everyone,' the officer repeated. 'In the meantime, I'll file a report for the theft of your money.' She pointed the end of her pen at Poppy. 'And you must promise me faithfully that you won't go looking for the thief yourself.'

'I promise,' Poppy said. And, at that precise moment in time, she meant every word.

16

Poppy had almost reached the stables when the sound of approaching hooves made her duck between two lorries. She watched crestfallen as Ned steered the carriage back to the yard, jumped from the cab and began unhooking Isadore and Roxie from the traces.

She'd missed her one opportunity to see Cloud, all because of George Blackstone. Yet again he'd come between her and her pony. It wasn't fair. Her face hardened, and she stalked back to the set in search of Scarlett.

Her scowl deepened when she saw her best friend chatting animatedly with Heidi Holland, but she attempted to paste on a smile as she joined them.

'Look at you two as thick as thieves.'

'Probably not the best analogy right now.' Heidi laughed, a musical tinkle that set Poppy's teeth on edge.

Ignoring Heidi, she turned to Scarlett. 'Have you spoken to PC Bodiam and Inspector Pearson?'

'Just PC Bodiam. The inspector was too busy asking Mrs Gordon for her autograph.'

'Did you tell her your suspicions about Blackstone?'

'Your suspicions, not mine. And no, I didn't.'

Heidi's eyes widened. 'Oo, what suspicions and about who? Do you know who the thief is?'

'No,' Poppy and Scarlett chimed.

'Oh, that's a shame.' Heidi rolled her sleeves up. As she did, the sun glinted on a bangle on her wrist.

'That's pretty,' Scarlett said. 'Is it silver?'

'Platinum. I treated myself when I was picked for this part. I've always wanted a Tiffany bracelet.'

'Wow. Tiffany? How much did that cost?'

'You know what they say. If you have to ask the price you probably can't afford it.'

Scarlett laughed. 'Haha, yes, you're probably right. It's gorgeous. Can I try it on?'

'Sure.' Heidi slipped the bangle off and handed it to Scarlett, who slid it over her hand and held her wrist up for them all to admire.

'One day I'd like to be able to afford lovely things like this,' she said wistfully. 'Maybe when I'm an Instagram influencer I'll be able to buy whatever I like. Hey Poppy, Heidi has more than two hundred thousand followers. She's been giving me some tips on how to increase my profile.'

'You should start an account for Cloud,' Heidi said to Poppy. 'He's such a darling, and he's going to be in the limelight when the series airs. Loads of free publicity. You'd be mad not to.'

'Poppy's not interested in that kind of thing, are you, Poppy?'

Poppy banished the image of the Christmas finale at Olympia from her head. OK, so perhaps she secretly liked the idea that Cloud might become famous, but she wasn't about to admit as much to Heidi.

'He's taught me so much,' Heidi continued, her eyes taking on a dreamy look. 'I've never been very interested in horses until now. But he's changed all that.'

'D'you think you'll keep riding once filming's over?' Scarlett asked.

'I'm not sure it'll be the same on another horse. I don't suppose…?'

'I'd sell him?' Poppy gave a derisive snort. 'Not for all the Tiffany bracelets in the world. What's wrong with you people? You think you can march in, throw your money around and buy whatever takes your fancy. It makes me so angry.'

Heidi's eyes widened. 'That's not actually what I was about to ask.' She stared at her hands for a moment, then stood. 'I think I might head for my trailer and re-read my lines for tomorrow.'

Once she was out of earshot, Scarlett rounded on Poppy. 'What did Heidi do to deserve that? Honestly, Poppy, you really are unbelievable sometimes.' She shook her head, and tore after Heidi, tugging the bangle from her wrist as she ran. 'Hey, Heidi, you forgot your bracelet!'

POPPY WAS STARING into the bottom of her glass of orange juice when PC Bodiam found her half an hour later.

'Have you got a minute?' the officer asked.

'Do I look like I'm doing anything?' Poppy snapped, then flushed a deep pink. 'Sorry, that came out wrong. It's not been a great morning. And being an extra is a lot less exciting than it sounds. It basically involves a lot of hanging around.'

'I'm sure.'

Poppy sat back in her seat. Was it her imagination or was PC Bodiam's voice lacking its usual warmth? Poppy placed her hands on the table. 'I might get another drink. Would you like one?'

PC Bodiam shook her head and peeled open her notebook. 'We've been talking to members of the cast and crew, which has proved... illuminating.' She paused, seeming to pick her words carefully. 'We've been told you were on the coach just before the thefts were discovered. Is that true?'

Poppy shifted in her seat. 'Well, yes. We were the ones who discovered the thefts.'

'Why didn't you mention that earlier?'

'I don't know. I suppose I didn't think it was important.'

'It's always important to know who was first on the scene of a crime.' PC Bodiam bent her head and jotted something in her notebook. 'Who's "we"?'

'Me and Scarlett.'

'And what were you doing on the coach?'

'Scarlett was fetching her phone.'

'Wasn't the coach supposed to be locked?'

Poppy shrugged. 'Don't ask me. Anyway, Scarlett went on first and came to find me when she realised her phone was missing. That's when I checked my purse and saw my birthday money had been stolen. And then Scarlett noticed Georgia's rucksack had been emptied onto the seat. I had a look through Georgia's stuff and saw her phone and purse were both missing, too.'

'You touched her bag and its contents?'

Poppy nodded.

'So your fingerprints will be all over them?'

A trickle of unease crawled down Poppy's spine. 'I guess. But you know we would never have stolen anything, right?'

PC Bodiam closed her notebook and slipped it back into her pocket. 'You have to understand that we have to act on all information we receive. We wouldn't be doing our job otherwise.'

Poppy frowned. 'Why would I steal my own money? And why would Scarlett steal her own phone? It doesn't make sense. Unless...' Her face cleared. 'Unless someone told you we did. Someone who wanted to take the heat off themselves. Someone like George Blackstone for example.'

PC Bodiam rubbed her nose. 'You know I'm not at liberty to divulge information about our inquiries.'

'Pinning the thefts on us would be very convenient for him, though, wouldn't it?' Poppy shook her head. 'He hates my guts, you know that.'

'There you go again, jumping to conclusions. No-one is accusing anyone of anything,' PC Bodiam said, not meeting Poppy's eye. 'I'd best be off. The guv'nor needs to be back at the nick by two.'

The officer navigated her way around the tables and chairs, heading towards Inspector Pearson and Heston Gray. She tapped her senior officer's shoulder and, heads bent, they were soon deep in conversation. At one point they glanced in Poppy's direction and she whipped out her phone and pretended to tap out a text while watching them from under her fringe. Eventually, they shook the director's hand, jumped in their patrol car and accelerated up the Claydon drive. Poppy stared balefully after them, feeling as though she'd just been accused of a crime she didn't commit.

17

P oppy scrolled mindlessly through her Instagram feed as she waited for Scarlett to return so she could fill her in on her unsettling conversation with PC Bodiam. But if she had hoped the arty black and white shots of other people's horses would take her mind off her predicament, she was wrong. She closed Instagram and opened Google, typing 'miscarriages of justice' into the search bar, and was soon engrossed in a myriad of stories of wrongful arrests and overturned convictions.

Because a miscarriage of justice was precisely what this was, she fumed. George Blackstone was accusing her and Scarlett of theft. PC Bodiam had no choice but to consider it as a possibility, she understood that. Because it was true: Poppy and Scarlett *had* been the last people on the coach. The only way they could show it wasn't them was by finding the real culprit. No, she corrected herself. She already knew who the real culprit was. She just needed *proof*.

But she would have to be careful. George Blackstone's reputation as a wily old fox preceded him. He was infamous across Dartmoor for his dodgy schemes and double-dealing ways. To outsmart him, she'd have to think like him. And she couldn't do it on her own, she needed Scarlett's help. It was a pity Scarlett wasn't her number one fan at the moment.

Poppy let out a long breath as she stood on tiptoes and scanned the car park and the tables and chairs in front of the catering truck for her best friend. But Scarlett was nowhere to be seen. She was probably enjoying a cosy chat with Heidi in her trailer. If two was company, Poppy brooded, three was definitely a crowd.

Even so, she needed to find the two girls so she could warn Scarlett that they were prime suspects for the thefts and apologise to Heidi for snapping.

She was trudging towards the trailers used by the cast when she spotted Krystal and Ned in a huddle with Kelvin and the chief cameraman. Their heads were bent over Kelvin's tatty copy of the script. Poppy hesitated. If they were here, they weren't with the horses. Which meant she could sneak over and see Cloud. Changing direction, she sloped off towards the stables.

CLOUD WAS STANDING at the back of his stable, but when Poppy called him, he whickered and stepped out of the gloom. She ruffled his forelock, and he nuzzled her pockets looking for a treat, nipping her when he realised she'd come empty-handed.

'Ow!' Poppy said, rubbing her forearm. 'That's very naughty,' she added, waggling her finger at him. It was also out of character. Cloud never bit, not even when she was doing up his girth. 'No more titbits for you if you're going to start that nonsense.' He turned his back to her and edged back into the shadows. Left staring at his rump, Poppy checked the coast was clear and let herself into the stable. He shifted his weight and swished his tail irritably.

'C'mon, Cloud,' she said, running a hand along his neck. 'I've managed to upset Scarlett already today. Don't you be cross with me, too.' She leaned against his solid bulk, not caring that her costume would end up covered in white hair. Cloud sighed and his stomach gurgled.

'Are you hungry?' Poppy stared around the loose box. The shavings bed was clean and had been banked around the back three walls, but the hay rack was empty and, Poppy suddenly noticed, the automatic water drinker was as dry as a bone. Spying a plastic switch on the vertical pipe that led to the drinker, she turned it ninety degrees and a trickle of water ran out. Cloud's ears pricked at the sound and he was by her side in an instant, his nose buried in the bowl as he slurped.

'You were thirsty, is that why you were so grumpy?' Poppy watched as he drank his fill then shook his head, shaking droplets all over her. His stomach rumbled again. 'Now for some hay.'

Poppy stood outside Cloud's stable, trying to remember where the hay barn was. Georgia had given her a guided tour of the yard years before, and if she recalled correctly, it was behind the tack room. She paused outside the feed room door. Cloud seemed so hungry she was tempted to mix him a hard feed, but she didn't know what the filming schedule was for the rest of the day, and if he needed to be ridden too soon after eating he could end up with colic. Some hay, she decided, would be fine.

The double doors to the barn were unlocked, and Poppy stood in the doorway and breathed in the sweet scent of meadow hay while her eyes adjusted to the dark. Spying an open bale, she helped herself to a section and headed back outside.

Out of nowhere, Krystal appeared, and Poppy dropped the hay in surprise.

'What do you think you're doing?' Krystal's tone was conversational, at odds with her choice of words.

Poppy scooped the hay up in her arms and hugged it to her chest. 'Oh, hello, Krystal. I didn't see you there. I popped by to say hello to Cloud. It's just as well I did, actually, because he didn't have any water, so I've turned his water drinker on. He'd finished all his hay, too, and I didn't think anyone would mind if I gave him a bit extra to keep him going until tea time.' Poppy, realising she was gabbling, flashed Krystal a smile. 'I hope that's all right.'

The older woman pressed her lips together. 'Of course it's all right. Ned must have turned the water off by accident. Don't worry, I'll make sure it doesn't happen again.'

'I don't want to drop him in it.'

'You haven't. But he needs to buck up his ideas. I won't put up with sloppy stable management.'

Cloud stuck his head over the stable door and, seeing Poppy clutching the hay, whinnied.

'You'd better give him that,' Kristal said, nodding at the hay. 'I would,' her face twisted into a smile, 'but whoever fixed the hay racks didn't spare a thought for people in wheelchairs.'

Poppy scuttled over to Cloud's stable and stood on tiptoes to drop the hay into the metal rack. Cloud pounced on it as if he hadn't been fed in days. 'Silly boy,' Poppy said, tweaking his ear. 'I'll see you tomorrow.' She joined Krystal outside. 'Shall I make sure the others have hay and water?'

'There's no need. Ned will be back any minute. He can do it.' Krystal drummed her fingers on the arm of her wheelchair. 'Look, there's no easy way to say this. I understand that you want to see Cloud, but please remember the stables are out of bounds to everyone except Ned and me. And that includes you. I need the horses' undivided attention if I am to prepare them for their scenes, and having you here is a distraction. Look what happened yesterday.'

'That wasn't me,' Poppy cried. 'Cloud's terrified of George Blackstone, that's why he had a meltdown.'

'So you said. But consider this from my point of view. My reputation depends on my horses doing what they are paid to do. I can't have them "having a meltdown" in the middle of a scene. Imagine what would have happened if Cloud had thrown Heidi off? If she'd been injured? It would have been a disaster. So please abide by clause seven in your contract and stay away until filming is finished.'

18

Charlie was painting a model aeroplane in the kitchen when Poppy stomped in a couple of hours later. He took one look at her face and set the plane on the table.

'What's the matter?'

'Nothing,' she said, reaching in the fridge for a can of lemonade.

'It doesn't look like nothing.'

'Where's Mum?'

'Popped over to Ashworthy for some eggs. We've got quiche for tea.'

Poppy took a long sip from the can and began opening and closing cupboard doors.

'What are you looking for?' Charlie asked.

'Chocolate.'

'Mum used the last bar to make chocolate chip cookies.'

'There are cookies?' Poppy lunged for the biscuit

tin, wrenched off the lid and peered inside. Apart from a few crumbs, it was empty.

'That was last week. We ate them all, remember?'

'But I need *chocolate!*' Poppy wailed.

Charlie dropped his brush in a jam jar of turpentine and stirred it around. 'I still have some Toblerone left over from my birthday. Would you like some of that?'

Poppy pulled up a chair and sat down heavily. 'I would.'

Charlie was back in seconds. He broke off three pieces of Toblerone and gave them to Poppy. She popped one in her mouth, closed her eyes and munched.

'I needed that,' she said, breaking off another piece and nibbling the corner. 'Thanks, little bro.'

'Are you going to tell me what's wrong?'

Poppy rubbed her face. 'Where do I start? I've upset Scarlett, I'm being accused of stealing, and to top it all, I'm banned from seeing my own pony.'

Charlie's eyebrows shot up. 'You're being accused of stealing? What d'you mean?'

Poppy found herself telling Charlie about the thefts on set, how George Blackstone was behind them all and how he must have pointed the finger at her.

'You're sure it was him?'

Poppy's eyes flashed. 'Of course I'm sure! Who else would it be? He's as crooked as they come and he's had a grudge against me for years.'

'I was only asking. There's no need to jump down my throat.'

'Sorry.' Poppy took another bite of chocolate and let

it dissolve on her tongue. The sugar helped sweeten the bitter taste the day had left in her mouth.

'Who's banned you from seeing Cloud?'

'Krystal. She needs his undivided attention during training and filming, and that means I'm not allowed near.'

Charlie blinked. 'She can do that, can she?'

'Apparently it's in the contract I signed.' Poppy held her hands up in surrender. 'I know, I should have read it, but I didn't, and there's nothing I can do about it now. He seems fine,' she said, brushing the memory of the dry water drinker aside. 'And he'll be home soon anyway, and we can put all this behind us.'

'And you and Scarlett are always falling out and making up again, so there's nothing unusual about that. Which just leaves George Blackstone and the fact that he's accusing you of being a thief.' Charlie picked up his brush, tapped it against the edge of the jam jar, wiped it off on a piece of kitchen roll and dipped it in a tin of olive-green enamel paint. Holding the plastic aeroplane still, he dabbed paint on its fuselage. 'What are you going to do about it?'

Poppy rested her chin in her hands. 'I don't know. I suppose I'll just have to hope the police believe me and not him.'

'That's a bit defeatist.'

'What would you do?'

'Are you up there again tomorrow?'

'No,' Poppy said. 'I'm not in any of the scenes.'

'Which rules out Plan A.'

Poppy frowned. 'Plan A?'

'You search through his belongings and find all the things he's stolen.' Charlie sucked the end of the paintbrush and pondered. 'It probably wouldn't work anyway. He's hardly likely to keep the evidence with him. Which leads me to Plan B. Is George Blackstone needed tomorrow?'

'Yes, they're shooting in the village again. The peasants and village children have both been told to show up. Blackstone is a peasant. Among other things,' she muttered. 'What's Plan B?'

Charlie put the final touches to the plane and held it to the light to inspect his handiwork. With a satisfied smile, he replaced it on the table. 'Just the markings to do now.'

'Charlie?' Poppy pressed.

Charlie snapped the lid back on the tin of paint and grinned at his sister. 'We cycle over to the Blackstone Farm while he's busy filming tomorrow and search the house until we find the loot.'

'I CAN'T BELIEVE you've talked me into this,' Poppy grumbled as they pushed their bikes down the Riverdale drive the following morning.

'You told Mum we're cycling over to Nethercote to see Jodie?' Charlie checked.

Poppy nodded. 'She offered to drive us over, but I said I needed the exercise.'

'And you've brought your phone and a couple of Freddie's dog chews?'

Poppy patted her pocket. 'And you've got your binoculars and camera?'

'Yep. We're all set. Don't worry, we'll soon clear your name.'

At the end of the drive, they jumped on their bikes and began pedalling towards the Blackstone farm. Beside her, Charlie was humming the Black Beauty theme tune. He was in his element, never happier than when setting off on an adventure, the riskier the better.

Poppy, on the other hand, was filled with misgivings. What if George Blackstone had decided he'd had enough of being an extra and had stayed at home? What if they couldn't find Scarlett's phone or Georgia's purse? What if a concerned neighbour heard the dogs barking and called the police?

As if reading her mind, Charlie gave her a smile. 'Don't worry, we'll be in and out in the blink of an eye.'

'But…'

'I'd rather regret the things I have done than the things that I haven't.'

Poppy tutted. 'You've been reading way too many memes.'

'It's true, though, isn't it? Remember what Dad always says. Fortune favours the brave.'

'I suppose. Look we're here. Why don't you keep watch at the end of the drive while I go and investigate?'

'No way. We're in this together.' Charlie jumped off his bike, wheeled it through the crumbling gateposts and propped it against the hedge so it couldn't be seen from the road.

'Is it a good idea to leave the bikes here? What if we need a quick getaway?'

'We'll have to run.' Charlie pulled his binoculars from his rucksack. 'Wait here while I check his Land Rover's not there.'

He was back in seconds, his eyes sparkling. 'Coast's clear,' he said. 'Ready?'

Poppy rubbed her clammy palms on her jeans. 'As I'll ever be.'

Charlie rubbed his hands together. 'What are we waiting for? Let's go and catch our thief.'

19

L ike Claydon Manor, the Blackstone farm looked even scruffier than Poppy remembered. A collection of semi-derelict barns and outbuildings surrounded the pitted, muddy farmyard. The farmhouse itself was a godforsaken place that wouldn't have looked out of place in a horror movie. Poppy shivered. They must be mad to come here. Stark, staring bonkers.

'C'mon Poppy,' Charlie said, tugging her sleeve. 'In and out in the blink of an eye, remember.'

Poppy followed Charlie past the old haybarn and the lean-to in which they'd once discovered a trapdoor leading to an underground air-raid shelter. The door was padlocked. Poppy gave the heavy-duty steel lock a hopeful tug, but it didn't budge. If Blackstone had hidden his spoils in the shed, they were out of luck.

The old hill farmer's two border collies were tied to a post inside the barn closest to the house. Seeing Charlie scamper over, Freddie's chews in his outstretched hand, the two dogs woofed a welcome and made a fuss of him, their tails wagging like crazy.

'They remembered me!' Charlie said, skipping back to Poppy with a grin on his face.

'You're probably the only person who ever brings them treats.'

Charlie ferreted around in his rucksack again and handed her a pair of woolly gloves.

'What are these for?'

'So you don't leave any fingerprints,' he said, pulling on a second pair.

Poppy paled. 'I've changed my mind. I want to go home.'

'Too late. We're here now.'

'But it's breaking and entering. What if we get caught?'

'The place is deserted. It'll be fine.'

Poppy pulled a face. When Charlie said, "it'll be fine" it was usually anything but. It was a case of Charlie's Famous Last Words, as they were known by the McKeevers. If Charlie commented on an empty motorway, a traffic jam inevitably awaited them around the next bend. If Charlie remarked on the fact that he hadn't fallen off his bike for a week, it went without saying that he'd soon come a cropper. And if Charlie assured her everything would be fine, based on past experiences Poppy could be forgiven for assuming the worst.

As if reading her mind, Charlie said, 'What's the worst that could happen?'

'Duh, George Blackstone could come home early,

find us in his house and call the police. We could be arrested, charged with burglary, found guilty and sentenced to time in a Young Offender Institution. I'd say that was probably about the worst.'

Charlie chortled. 'You're such a pessimist. If you're that worried, we won't go into the house. We'll just look through the windows. Deal?'

Poppy nodded. That sounded more like nosiness than breaking and entering. And since when had being nosy been a crime? 'Deal,' she said.

Happy that the dogs were still gnawing at their chews, they crossed over to the nearest window and peered in. The glass was so filthy it was hard to see anything, but gradually Poppy made out an old pine dresser, a table and, directly in front of them, a grimy sink.

'The kitchen,' she said.

'Yuck.' Charlie wrinkled his nose and pointed to the sink, which was filled with dirty pots and pans. On the other side of the window, a bluebottle threw itself at the glass pane, desperate to escape.

Poppy scanned the cluttered kitchen counters and table looking for anything out of place, such as a brand-new iPhone or a purse. But all she could make out were piles of papers, more dirty cups and plates, a half-empty bottle of whisky and an overflowing ashtray.

'I can't see anything, can you?' she said.

Charlie shook his head. 'But I'll take a couple of pictures anyway. We can enlarge them on the laptop and take a closer look once we're home.'

They moved onto the next window and gazed into George Blackstone's dining room. As in the kitchen, the dining room table was buckling under the weight of clutter. On an old desk in the corner bags of coppers were piled in a pyramid, but there were no notes, and no phones or purses.

'The lounge must be around the front of the house,' Charlie said. He snapped a couple of photos and beckoned Poppy to follow.

She stared through the grubby glass, taking in the solitary armchair in front of the fire, the once cream walls now yellow with nicotine, and the tracks of mud on the threadbare rug. More clutter was piled on a dark wooden sideboard, and there was another bottle of whisky and a dirty glass on a small table to the side of the armchair. Poppy pictured the old farmer in his chair in front of the fire, plotting his nefarious schemes.

'Can't see anything,' she said, turning away. 'He's obviously hidden it all. Come on, let's go.'

'There's one more window we haven't checked.' Charlie dipped his head. 'The one to the right of the back door.'

Finding their way was blocked by two old concrete coal bunkers, they retraced their steps to the back of the house. Pushing past Charlie, who was hovering by the back door, Poppy cupped her hands to her forehead and squinted into the room. Blackstone's boot room, by the look of it. And it was as gloomy and squalid as the rest of the house. A handful of filthy coats hung from hooks along one wall, mud-encrusted boots lay abandoned on the old flagstone floor, and a ceramic sink was cracked and black with grime. Poppy grimaced and stepped away from the window. She'd seen enough. The sooner they left, the better. As she turned to go, she cast one last look inside the window.

Her hand flew to her chest, and she staggered back in shock.

A face was peering back at her through the murky glass.

'Charlie! What on earth are you doing in there? You nearly gave me a heart attack!'

'The door wasn't locked,' he said, his face so close to the window that his breath clouded the glass. 'So it's not breaking and entering.'

'Just entering,' Poppy grumbled, as she marched through the back door to fetch him. 'Seriously, Charlie, we need to go.'

'All right, I'm coming,' he said, appearing in a doorway at the back of the kitchen.

A sudden noise outside the house made them start, and they stared at each other in horror.

'What was that?'

'It sounded like a car.' Poppy clapped her hand over her mouth. 'Oh my God, what if Blackstone's come home early? We need to leave. Now!'

'It's too late. If we go outside he'll see us,' Charlie said. He lunged forwards and pulled the door closed. 'We'll hide in here,' he said, disappearing back into the boot room.

For a moment, Poppy faltered, her eyes darting between the back door and the boot room. The sound of the approaching engine was growing louder by the second. Maybe she'd have time to sprint over to the barn and hide. But there was no way she was leaving Charlie on his own in the house. Her mind made up, she dashed after her brother.

Poppy crashed into the boot room and stopped in her tracks when she realised there was no sign of Charlie.

'Where are you?' she said, an edge of exasperation creeping into her voice.

One of the coats on the rack started shaking and emitted a gurgle of laughter. Charlie was hiding behind a scruffy wax coat, his feet in two enormous wellies. He poked his head out and sneezed. Poppy held a finger to her lips. 'Shush!'

'Sorry, it's a bit fusty in here,' he said, disappearing back behind the coat. Poppy took a deep breath and, holding her nose, slipped behind a shabby tweed hacking jacket.

The engine noise was now so loud it must be right outside. A car door slammed, and footsteps approached the back door. Footsteps, accompanied by whistling. Cheery, tuneful whistling that Poppy had heard before. Most days, in fact. An image of Doug the postman crunching up the Riverdale drive in his red van popped into her head. When the letterbox snapped open, followed by the thud of mail dropping on the doormat, Poppy knew she was right. She slipped out from behind the tweed jacket and peered around the side of the window.

Doug was making his way back to his van, hands in pockets and still whistling to himself.

'It's Doug, the postman,' she said, releasing the breath she'd been holding.

'Are you sure?' came a muffled reply.

'Of course I'm sure you twit. He's just going.' But before Doug opened the van door, he turned, stared up at the house and said, 'Nice to see you've been spoiling the dogs for a change.' Poppy shrank back into the shadows, as nervy as a stable cat, but not before she glimpsed Doug giving whoever he was talking to a double thumbs up. He jumped in the van and sped back down the drive.

Charlie crept out from behind the coats. 'Who was he talking to?'

'I don't know. No-one else lives here, do they?'

'Blackstone's mum?'

'She must have been dead thirty years.'

'The ghost of Blackstone's mum?' Charlie whispered with a ghoulish smile.

'Don't be ridiculous,' Poppy said, but not before a shiver ran down her spine.

'It couldn't be Shelley, could it?'

'No, she's still in prison, and Hope's in Canada. He

must have been talking to himself. Come on, I've had enough of this place. Let's go.'

Back outside, they stared up at the house.

'Where was he looking?' Charlie asked.

'The window above the back door. But there's no-one there.'

'Just an all-seeing eye,' Charlie said, nodding to himself.

'What d'you mean?'

'There's a camera, right above the door. Look.'

If the thought of the ghost of Blackstone's old mum sent a shiver down Poppy's spine, the sight of a small CCTV camera blinking away above her head was enough to make her quake with terror.

Because it would have recorded every single second of them sneaking around the farmyard and creeping into the house. It didn't matter that they were doing it with the best intentions. There was no getting away from it - they looked as guilty as hell.

POPPY'S THIGHS were burning as she pedalled furiously along the lane, trying to put as much distance as possible between them and the Blackstone farm. It was only when she realised Charlie had fallen far behind that she stopped in a layby and waited for him to catch up.

'We're going to have to tell Mum,' she said, as he reached her.

'Why?'

'Because we've broken the law. And when Black-stone checks his camera and sees us on his land, he's going to phone the police. It would be better if we told them first.'

'We didn't steal anything.'

'That's not the point. We shouldn't have been there.' Poppy hit her handlebar with the heel of her hand. 'Urghh! Why did I listen to you in the first place? I knew it was a terrible idea.'

'You wanted to clear your name,' Charlie reminded her.

'And I've done that, have I?' She shook her head in exasperation. 'Of course I haven't. All I've done is make things a thousand times worse. The police are probably at ours now, waiting to arrest us both.'

'Now you're being silly. We only left Blackstone's place ten minutes ago. There's no way they'd be there already.'

Poppy stared at her brother. 'Aren't you worried?'

'Nah. The police have bigger fish to fry than nicking two kids for mooching around a skanky old farmyard.'

'You think?'

'And anyway, you're supposing Blackstone even bothers to check his CCTV. Everything's exactly as he left it. He's not going to trawl through hours and hours of footage unless something has been stolen. You'd be telling Mum and landing us in trouble for nothing. Why?'

'Because it's the right thing to do.'

'And then Mum'll be in an awkward position. Dob

in her own children or not dob us in and be our partner in crime?'

'What would you do?'

'I'd keep schtum. It's a no-brainer.'

———————

'Hello, sweetheart. Nice bike ride?' Caroline said as Poppy clumped in through the back door twenty minutes later.

'Yeah, it was good, thanks,' Poppy said, keeping her gaze on the floor as she heeled off her trainers.

'Where did you go?'

'Oh, just down to Hope's old cottage and back.'

'I'd have thought you'd have headed onto the moor.'

'It's a nice quiet lane, and Charlie wanted to practice riding with no hands.'

Caroline raised her eyes to the ceiling. 'Of course he did.' She reached in a cupboard for a couple of mugs. 'Hot chocolate?'

'I might head straight up to my room. I need to make a start on my English Lit essay.'

'I can't tempt you with one of these?' her stepmum said, waving a plate of chocolate brownies under her nose. 'They're still warm.'

Poppy wavered.

'Come on, Poppy. We haven't sat down and had a proper chat for ages. I'm sure the essay can wait until this afternoon.'

'Oh all right then.' Poppy pulled out a chair while Caroline busied herself making their drinks.

'I just wanted to check everything's OK,' she said, handing Poppy a mug. 'Only you seemed a little quiet when you came home yesterday.'

Poppy wrapped her fingers around her drink. 'I'd had a bit of a bust-up with Scarlett. We've made up now.'

She'd texted *SORRY FOR BEING AN IDIOT* to Scarlett the previous evening and had been relieved when a reply had pinged straight back.

I know you can't help it. Being an idiot, I mean! with a laughing emoji. *But, seriously, you don't have to be quite so judgy all the time, you know. Heidi's lovely. She didn't deserve to get an earful.*

Poppy had felt as though she'd been told off by her favourite teacher, but at least Scarlett was talking to her.

'What was it about?' Caroline asked. Then, seeing Poppy's blank expression, 'the bust-up?'

Poppy massaged her temple. 'I thought Heidi Holland wanted to buy Cloud so I gave her a piece of my mind.'

'Oh dear,' Caroline said, laughing.

'But I got the wrong end of the stick, apparently, and she wasn't asking that at all. I don't know why I over-reacted. I'm just feeling a bit... lost without him.'

'He'll be home before you know it. Filming finishes at the end of the week, doesn't it?'

'It's supposed to. But they're so behind schedule, who knows?'

'And is that all it is?' Caroline asked.

Poppy was silent.

'Poppy?'

Keep schtum, Charlie had said. George Blackstone might never watch his CCTV. But Caroline's gaze felt hot on Poppy's skin, and suddenly the urge to confess was impossible to ignore.

She took a deep breath. 'There is something, yes.'

21

'We went to the Blackstone farm to find evidence that George Blackstone is the one who's been stealing everyone's belongings,' Poppy told her stepmum.

'Pardon?' Caroline said, her mug halfway to her mouth.

'That's not all. The back door wasn't locked, so we went inside, too. Then the postman came, so we hid in the boot room, and when we came out, we saw a CCTV camera, so Blackstone will know we've been in his house and will probably have us arrested.' The words tumbled out before Poppy could stop them.

'You went inside his house?'

'I'm sorry. I know it was stupid, but it seemed the only way.'

'The only way of what?'

'I told you. Of proving Blackstone is the purse thief.'

'Oh, Poppy.' Caroline set her mug on the table and ran a hand through her hair. 'What were you thinking?'

Poppy slid down her chair and looked sidelong at her stepmum. 'I don't think I was.'

Caroline stood, walked stiffly to the bottom of the stairs and bellowed, 'Charlie! Down here now, please.'

One look at his sister's face told Charlie all he needed to know.

'What did you tell her for?' he cried.

'I don't like lying.'

'That's never stopped you before. What about that time you -'

'Charlie, that's enough.' Caroline faced them, her hands on her hips. 'Whose idea was this?'

'Mine,' Poppy said in a monotone. 'I convinced Charlie to come with me even though he said it was a stupid idea.'

'Is this true?' Caroline asked Charlie.

He made to speak, but Poppy beat him to it. 'It is, I promise.'

'I can't believe how reckless you've been. What if George Blackstone had found you in his house? The man has a vicious temper. Look what he did to Cloud. And Jenny. And those poor dogs.' Caroline marched into the hallway and returned with the phone.

'What are you doing?' Charlie said.

'Calling the police to tell them what's happened.' The two children watched in silence as Caroline stabbed a number into the handset and waited for someone to answer. 'Yes, hello. I would like to report an… incident. Yes, of course. It's Caroline McKeever of Riverdale, Waterby. Oh, hello, Claire, I thought I recognised your voice. Yes, everything's fine. It's just…'

Poppy perched on the edge of her chair as Caroline briefed PC Bodiam on their latest escapade. Straining to hear the officer's response, all she could hear was a faint buzz.

'At least it's PC Bodiam,' she whispered to Charlie, but he shook his head and looked away.

'I see. Yes, I agree. I'll tell them. Thank you, Claire. I really appreciate it.'

Caroline ended the call and drummed her fingers on the table. 'PC Bodiam has logged the incident and said she will need to raise the matter with her inspector.'

Poppy's insides turned to ice. Even Charlie was watching Caroline with a look of horror on his face.

'For a charge of burglary, the police would have to prove that when you entered George Blackstone's house as trespassers, you intended to steal, assault someone or commit criminal damage.'

'Which we really didn't,' Poppy said earnestly. 'We just wanted to prove he'd stolen my money and Scarlett's phone.'

'PC Bodiam said she warned you against taking matters into your own hands when she saw you at Claydon Manor yesterday.'

Poppy hung her head.

'She's spent the morning working on the case. It turns out that two wallets and a purse were stolen from the catering truck on the first day of filming. A day when George Blackstone wasn't even on set.'

'Doesn't mean he couldn't have sneaked over there,' Charlie said.

'There you go again,' Caroline tutted. 'Blackstone was, in fact, at the livestock market in Holsworthy nearly forty miles away when the items were stolen. At least three witnesses saw him there.'

Poppy fiddled with the hem of her jumper. 'So it might not have been him.'

'PC Bodiam said she's ruled him out of her inquiries.'

'She could be wrong.'

'She has years of experience as a police officer. She's probably investigated more cases than you've had hot dinners. If she says it wasn't George Blackstone, it wasn't George Blackstone. You've been spying on an innocent man.'

'Innocent? Hardly,' Charlie said under his breath.

'On this occasion he was innocent,' Caroline said.

Poppy buried her face in her hands. 'I'm sorry, Mum. I really thought it must have been him.' An unwelcome thought occurred to her. 'He's going to be so mad when he sees us on CCTV snooping around his farm if he hasn't done anything wrong. What d'you think he'll do?'

'PC Bodiam said trespass on its own was not a criminal offence. He could still take civil action, but that would mean putting his hands in his pockets and paying a lawyer, which she felt was unlikely.'

'Him being as tight as they come,' Charlie said, brightening. 'Does that mean we're not in any trouble?'

'Not so fast, young man.' Caroline's lips thinned. 'You are in a whole heap of trouble. I'm grounding you both for a week.'

'Grounding us?' Charlie cried. 'That's not fair!'

'A whole week? But I won't be able to see Cloud,' Poppy wailed. 'And what about Black Beauty? I'm needed on set!'

'I'm sorry Poppy, but you should have thought of that before you went sneaking off to George Blackstone's. You've left me with no choice.'

———

POPPY BURIED her head in her hands and groaned. 'Grounded for a week. I can't believe it.'

'It completely sucks,' Charlie agreed. 'And in the Easter holidays, too. It's a disaster.'

They'd trudged upstairs to Poppy's room, Caroline's rebuke still ringing in their ears. Poppy's throat felt sore when she swallowed as if she was getting a cold. But deep down, she knew the only thing she was suffering from was shame. They'd been so stupid. Caroline had every right to be angry.

Magpie was snoring at the end of her bed. She reached out to tickle him under the chin. He opened one eye, then the other, stretched, jumped down and stalked out of the room, his tail flicking with displeasure at the interruption to his beauty sleep.

'Even Magpie hates me,' Poppy said disconsolately.

'I don't hate you,' Charlie said. 'I think you're mad for 'fessing up to Mum, but you took the rap for me. You didn't have to do that. It was my idea.'

'Yeah, well.' Poppy gave him a wan smile. 'You were only trying to help.'

Charlie began pacing the room. 'We may have ruled out Blackstone, but the thief's still at large. Who else could it be?'

'I don't know, and I don't care. We're not supposed to get involved. You heard Mum.'

But it was as if she hadn't spoken. 'I have had one idea,' he continued. 'I was googling ways to catch a thief last night, and I found this stuff called theft detection powder for sale on eBay. You dust it over a thing that might be stolen, like a wallet, for example, and when someone touches the wallet, the powder reacts with their skin and leaves a purple stain on them. It helps you catch a thief purple-handed.' He guffawed at his own joke. 'We could order some.'

'Don't even think about it,' Poppy warned. 'We're in enough trouble as it is. Do you want to be grounded for the entire Easter holidays, because I don't. I'm afraid it's time we left the detective work to the police.'

22

Poppy spent the weekend being a model daughter. She emptied the dishwasher, laid the table and took out the rubbish without being asked. She helped Caroline weed the vegetable garden and even offered to clean the bathroom, a job they both hated.

'I could get used to this,' Caroline said, as Poppy brought her breakfast in bed on Sunday morning. Toast, Caroline's favourite marmalade and a mug of builders' tea, strong enough to stand a spoon in, just how she liked it.

'I wanted to show you I really am sorry for going behind your back,' Poppy said. And it was true. If she could turn back the clock she would in a heartbeat.

But making amends to Caroline was only part of the reason. She also hoped that keeping busy would stop her obsessing about Cloud. Because she missed him more than she thought possible. Without him, she felt adrift, incomplete. Every time she stepped out of the back door or glanced out of her bedroom window expecting to see him, a wave of disappointment washed over her as she remembered he'd gone.

She'd taken to texting Georgia four or five times a day, asking if he was OK. At first, Georgia had been mildly amused by Poppy's texts and had even snuck into the indoor school a couple of times to take photos of Cloud's training sessions.

In the first photo she'd sent, Ned was lungeing Cloud as Krystal watched, and in the second Cloud was bowing, his near foreleg stretched out in front of him while his off-foreleg was bent at the knee. But it was the third photo that mesmerised Poppy. Cloud was on a lunge rein again, but this time Krystal held the other end in her left hand. In her right was a raised lunge whip. Georgia had managed to catch Cloud mid-rear, his hind legs bent low to the ground and his front legs striking out in front of him. His nostrils were flared, and his gaze was fixed on the tip of the whip. He looked like a wild mustang, fierce and untamed.

Poppy had pored over the photo for ages, tracing the crest of his neck with her index finger, marvelling at his strength and grace. Hoping, if she was honest, that he wouldn't remember that particular trick once he was home.

By Sunday evening, Georgia had grown bored of Poppy's texts and had told her in no uncertain terms to get a life. With her only link to Cloud broken and no prospect of seeing him for at least another five days, Poppy had barely touched her roast dinner.

'You're not sickening for something are you?' Caroline said, jumping to her feet and feeling Poppy's forehead.

'No, I'm fine. Don't fuss.'

'So tell me what's wrong.'

'It's Cloud's first big scene tomorrow, and I won't be there to watch him.'

'You didn't tell me.'

'I only found out just before tea. Heidi told Scarlett who texted me because she thought I'd want to know. It's the scene where Miss Flora and Miss Jessie ride Merrylegs and Black Beauty onto the moor for a picnic and come face to face with the highwaymen.'

'I can't remember there being any highwaymen in the book,' Caroline said.

'There weren't any.' Poppy scraped her uneaten dinner into the bin. 'Cloud has to rear and gallop away while Isadore, that's the horse playing Black Beauty, stays and protects the girls. Scarlett says they don't need any extras tomorrow, but she's going along to watch anyway.'

'And you'd like to go, too?'

'But she can't watch her pony making his stunt debut because you grounded her. Even though all she was trying to do was solve a crime. It's not *fair*,' Charlie grumbled.

Poppy cleared the rest of the plates while Caroline took an apple pie out of the oven.

'Not for me, thanks. I'm going to bed,' Poppy said.

'But it's only eight o'clock. And you love apple pie.'

'I'm not hungry.'

'She's pining,' Charlie said. 'Can't you see? She'll probably have starved to death by the end of the week.'

'Don't be ridiculous.' Caroline handed him a slice of pie and a jug of cream. She was quiet for a moment, gazing out of the kitchen window while rubbing her earlobe. Eventually, she turned back to Poppy and said, 'I have to say I've been very impressed with the way you've behaved this weekend. You didn't sulk or throw a strop…'

'There wasn't much point. I knew we shouldn't have gone.'

'… and you do seem to have learnt your lesson.' Caroline fixed Charlie with a look. 'I'm not so sure the same can be said for your brother.'

Charlie glanced at Poppy, who raised an eyebrow and gave a tiny nod.

'I've definitely learnt my lesson, Mummy. There's no way I'll ever be setting foot on the Blackstone farm ever, *ever* again.'

Poppy smiled to herself. Charlie only called Caroline Mummy when he wanted something, and it usually worked.

On cue, Caroline's expression softened. 'I'm glad to hear it. In that case, I think two days' grounding is sufficient. As from tomorrow morning, you're officially free. As long as you promise you won't try any more funny business.'

Poppy crossed the kitchen in a couple of strides and threw her arms around her stepmum. 'I promise! Thank you *so* much.' She grinned. 'I'll be able to watch Cloud strut his stuff after all.'

'Can I come, too?' Charlie pleaded.

'I don't mind taking you if Mum says it's OK?' Poppy looked inquiringly at Caroline.

'I don't see why not.'

Charlie whooped, and Poppy's tummy rumbled.

'I've changed my mind,' she said. 'I think I can manage a slice of apple pie, after all.'

'Remember, Heidi told Scarlett it's OK for us to watch the filming as long as we're deathly quiet and stay well out of shot,' Poppy told Charlie as they pushed their bikes up the Claydon drive the following morning.

'This is so exciting,' Charlie said, his eyes on stalks. 'Scarlett must be mad, not wanting to come.'

'Barney offered her an extra shift at the shop, and she needed the money. She still hasn't told her mum her phone's been stolen. Look, that's Krystal the horse master with Kelvin, the assistant director,' Poppy said, pointing towards the pair, who were chatting by the costume truck. 'They must be discussing today's scene.'

Poppy pointed out other members of the cast and crew as they made their way onto the set.

'You know everyone,' Charlie said, his eyes wide.

'Yes, well, I'm an old hand now. Want to meet a TV star?'

'Duh, obvs.'

Poppy led him over to Heidi Holland, who was sitting alone at a table outside the catering truck, her eyes fixed on her phone. Hearing footsteps, she slipped the phone into her pocket, her eyes darting around nervously. When she saw it was them, her frown lines disappeared, and she tittered.

'I thought you were Kelvin. I'm supposed to be learning my lines, not checking my Instagram feed. I stuffed up during rehearsals. So if anyone asks…'

'We'll tell them we were helping you practise,' Poppy said. 'I'm glad you're here. I wanted to apologise for the other day. I was out of order.'

'That's all right. It must be hard seeing someone else riding your pony.'

'It is.' Poppy smiled briefly. 'I didn't realise how much I'd miss him. How is he?'

Heidi drew a circle in the air with her index finger. 'He's been running rings around Krystal and Ned.'

'That doesn't sound good.'

Heidi screwed up her face, then grinned. 'I mean he's *literally* running rings around them. You know, when they put him on a super-long dog lead and make him canter around in a circle while they stand in the middle with a ginormous whip.'

'You mean they've been lungeing him?' Poppy said.

'If that's what it's called. Ned always does it before one of Cloud's scenes. Krystal says it concentrates his mind because she can't risk any more crazy behaviour. Afterwards, he has a bath to wash all the sweat off and goes into make-up to have his nose painted pink. Ned's probably lungeing him now. We've got a big scene today.'

'That's why we're here. We're going to watch,' Charlie said. 'Plus the fact that I wanted to see some real-life television stars.' He smiled disingenuously. 'How much do you earn?'

'Charlie! It's rude to ask people about money,' Poppy said, mouthing an apology to Heidi.

'Only it must be loads, 'cos that was the new generation iPhone, wasn't it? Same as Scarlett's.'

Heidi shifted in her seat. 'I upgraded when I won the part. Thought I'd treat myself.'

Poppy tilted her head to one side. Heidi had treated herself to an expensive platinum bracelet, too. Funny how she seemed to be rolling in money just when belongings were going missing from the set. A coincidence... or not?

'Nice work if you can get it,' Charlie was saying. ''Cos Poppy said you've only had bit parts until now.'

'No I didn't,' Poppy said, elbowing her brother in the ribs and trying to ignore the flame-red flush that was racing up her neck. 'I was talking about the actress playing Heidi's sister, not Heidi herself, idiot!'

Charlie frowned. 'I'm sure you said Heidi.'

'I didn't,' Poppy said through gritted teeth. 'Heidi's *sister*. Honestly, you never listen.' She grimaced at Heidi. 'Brothers! Who'd have 'em? We'll leave you in peace.' She grabbed Charlie's arm so tightly he gave a little yelp of surprise. 'And don't forget to break a leg,' she added, marching off, Charlie half-running by her side.

23

'Thanks for nothing,' Poppy muttered, once they were out of earshot.

'I was only telling the truth,' Charlie said with a pained expression. He rubbed his arm. 'You did say Heidi.'

'I know, but a bit of tact and diplomacy wouldn't go amiss. You really dropped me in it. Heidi already thinks I hate her.'

He looked around. 'Which famous person are we going to insult now?'

'No-one. You can make amends by keeping a lookout while I say hello to Cloud.'

Charlie nodded and skipped along beside her as she strode towards the stable block. When they reached the first loose box, she stopped. 'Wait here and give a low whistle if you see Krystal coming. I need to make sure Ned's out of the way.'

He nodded, crossed his arms and leaned against the weatherboarded building. Poppy crept past the stables, looking in each as she passed. Roxy whickered when she saw her, and Poppy rubbed the narrow white stripe down the middle of the chestnut mare's face. It was only when the edges smudged, leaving a daub of white on her hands, that she realised it wasn't a stripe at all - it had been painted on.

'Nothing around here is as it seems,' she murmured to herself, rubbing her hand on her jeans.

Her pulse quickened as she approached Cloud's stable, and she ran over, calling his name. But it was empty. Ned must be lungeing him in the indoor school.

From the angle of the photos Georgia had sent her, Poppy guessed the older girl had taken them from the viewing gallery. As long as she was quiet, Ned would never know she was there. Jogging over to the door, Poppy tried the handle, breathing a sigh of relief as it opened smoothly. She slunk in, keeping her back to the wall.

As she neared the wall that separated the viewing area from the arena, she crouched down and listened. A faint sound like the swishing of a tail was followed by a voice crying, 'Up! UP!'

Poppy clasped the top of the wall and pulled herself up, centimetre by centimetre. As she stuck her head above the parapet, a gunshot splintered the air, and she dropped to the ground like a stone, her heart crashing in her chest.

The gun fired again, and the voice shouted 'Up!' A horse whinnied. Not Cloud, she'd know his call anywhere. 'Up, damn you!' the voice cried again. It was Ned, Poppy was sure of it. Though her legs felt as weak as jelly, she risked another look. Isadore was standing in the centre of the school pawing the ground, the whites of his eyes brilliant against his glossy black coat. Standing in front of him with a lunge whip in one hand was Ned. He took a step towards the horse, lifted his arms in an upwards movement and shouted, 'Up!'

Isadore snaked his head towards the young stunt rider, his teeth bared. Ned staggered backwards. His whip arm vertical, he brought it down with a slicing movement and another crack reverberated around the high-ceilinged building. A small sonic boom, made as the whip travelled faster than the speed of sound. Not a gun at all.

This time Isadore did rear, his front hooves waving in the air less than a metre from Ned's face. The black stallion walked forwards on his hindlegs as Ned walked backwards. When Ned stopped, Isadore stopped, too, dropping back down to the ground. Poppy was transfixed as Ned threw his arms up again, shouting, Up!' This time the tip of the whip lashed Isadore's ear, whether by accident or design Poppy couldn't be sure. The horse squealed, turned his back on Ned and kicked out with both back legs. Ned caught a glancing blow on his thigh, and he let off a stream of expletives as Isadore careered around the school, his silken mane and tail rippling like flags on a blustery day. It would have been a joyful sight if it hadn't been for his heaving flanks, sweat-darkened neck and a small nick on his ear.

A rush of air as the horse hurtled past her brought Poppy to her senses, and she threw herself to the ground. Ned was still swearing as she crept out of the school, shut the door and leaned against it until her heart rate had steadied.

Charlie was waiting where she'd left him. He took one look at her pale face, and his eyes widened. 'You look like you've seen a ghost.'

'Not a ghost.'

'Cloud?'

She shook her head. 'Isadore. That's the horse playing Black Beauty. Ned was... schooling him.'

Is that what it was? Poppy knew nothing about training stunt horses so felt in no position to pass judgement on what she'd seen. But there had been no kind words, no pat on the neck, no acknowledgement that Isadore had done what was asked of him. No carrot, just a big stick. And Ned's harsh tone and abrasive behaviour had been mirrored back at him when the stallion kicked out and galloped off. It hadn't been easy to watch.

'Where *is* Cloud?' Charlie said.

Poppy's shoulders sagged. 'I don't know.'

THEY FOUND him in the horse walker behind the indoor school, pacing round and round. The vast metal contraption had reminded Poppy of an industrial-sized rotary washing line the first time she'd seen it. She knew they were a common sight on professional yards and were useful for rehabilitating horses coming back from injury. Still, she would have bet her last pound that Cloud would have preferred a hack than circling like a caged hamster on a wheel. She jogged around with him until she was out of breath and dizzy, then clutched the steel link fencing and talked to him every time he passed.

'Uh oh,' Charlie said. 'That Krystal woman is on her way over.'

Poppy's first instinct was to flee. But she ignored it and stood her ground. The horse walker, the scene in the indoor school, the day she'd found Cloud without hay or water all played on her mind. She couldn't ignore them any longer.

'Poppy,' Krystal said evenly. 'I thought we'd agreed the horses were out of bounds?'

'You agreed,' Poppy said.

'And you signed the contract,' Krystal answered. 'But no matter.' Her gaze slid to Charlie, who hooked his thumbs in the pockets of his jeans and stared back.

His open defiance gave Poppy courage. 'I'm glad I've seen you, Krystal. I wondered why Cloud was in the horse walker. I would have exercised him for you if you'd asked.'

'I told you. For my training methods to be effective, I need owners out of the picture.'

Poppy bit her lip. 'Going round and round in circles isn't training.'

'You're right, of course. But I'm afraid Ned's to blame for this.' She waved her hands at the horse walker.

'Ned? But he's with Isadore in the indoor school.'

'I asked him to lunge Cloud before his training

session with Isadore. Unfortunately, the only thing Ned's good at is cutting corners. I'll see that it doesn't happen again.'

'Thank you.'

With the press of a button, Krystal stopped the horse walker. Spying Cloud's lead rope pooled on the floor, Poppy picked it up and said, 'I'll get him for you.'

Without waiting for an answer, she let herself into the horse walker and approached Cloud. As she held the lead rope towards him, he threw his head up and took a step backwards, his rump colliding with the partition. 'Hey, it's only me,' she said, running her hand along his neck. Feeling him relax under her touch, she kissed his nose and clipped the lead rope onto his headcollar. He pushed gently against her, his cheek against hers, and, in a voice suddenly scratchy with unshed tears, she whispered in his ear. 'Not long now, baby. Then you'll be home.'

24

T he picnic was to be filmed on the bank of a small moorland stream half a mile north of Claydon Manor. Poppy and Charlie followed the cast and crew as they made their way to the location and found a quiet corner behind the make-up girls to watch the action.

Seeing them, Heidi ambled over and threw Poppy her Ted Baker backpack. 'Be an angel and keep an eye on it for me?'

Poppy caught the bag. 'Sure.'

'We appear to be missing two horses,' Heston said, looking around. 'Ah, no, here they are.'

Poppy turned to see Ned leading Cloud and Isadore along the track towards them. One as black as night, the other sparkling white apart from his pewter-grey dapples. A breath caught in her throat. They looked magical.

'How come you never get Cloud that clean?' Charlie said under his breath, breaking the spell.

Heston ordered everyone to their stations. Ned led Cloud and Isadore to a nearby stile and tied them up loosely.

'It's made of balsawood, so it breaks when the horses are frightened by the highwaymen,' said one of the make-up girls, who was standing nearby. 'Realistic, isn't it?' The make-up girl darted forwards, wielding powder and a brush as Heidi and her on-screen sister settled themselves on a tartan picnic rug. In front of them was enough food to feed a small army. Pork pies, cherry tomatoes, Cornish pasties and chicken drumsticks. A fruit cake, scones and strawberries.

'How are they supposed to have carried all that here?' Charlie whispered.

'Doesn't matter. It's artistic licence,' Poppy whispered back.

'Quiet on set!' Heston called. 'Roll sound. Roll camera!'

'Scene thirty-five, take one.' Kelvin slammed the clapperboard shut.

'And... action!'

The whirr of the cameras was the cue for the two young actresses to spring into their roles. They chatted animatedly as they passed each other plates of food and spooned cream onto scones. From the odd word Poppy caught, they seemed to be talking about the reward their father was offering for the capture of the highwaymen.

The series was so far removed from the original book that Poppy was beginning to wonder how they dared to call it Black Beauty at all. When she'd said as much to Caroline, her stepmum had laughed and said, 'Trouble is, everyone expects high-octane adventure these days. You can't blame the production company for wanting to inject a little drama into the story.'

'Are you mad? Beauty's life was one big drama. He was caught in a stable fire, saved the lives of Squire Gordon and his groom, nearly died after catching a chill, fell and scarred his knees, was sold as a cab horse and was worked until he literally dropped. Is that not dramatic enough for you?'

Caroline had held up her hands. 'Don't blame me. I happen to agree with you. But there's nothing wrong with Anna Sewell's story being the inspiration for this show, is there? It means a whole new generation will fall in love with Black Beauty and will probably go on to read the book.'

She supposed her stepmum was right. She usually was. Poppy was self-aware enough to know that she had a tendency to be a teeny bit self-righteous and that life was never black and white. As long as the show conveyed Anna Sewell's anti-cruelty message Poppy would be happy.

'Cut!' Heston yelled.

Poppy nudged Charlie. 'What happened?'

'Heidi forgot her lines.'

'Oops.' Poppy sat cross-legged, Heidi's backpack in her lap, and played with a black leather tassel, rolling it between her finger and thumb. Kelvin scurried over to Heidi and waved the script under her nose. Heidi frowned as she read and then nodded and gave him the thumbs up.

'It must be impossible to remember all those words. It's bad enough remembering a single spelling,' Charlie said.

'Shush. They're doing another take.'

This time Heidi reeled off her lines without a hitch. Behind the two girls, Cloud and Isadora waited patiently for their big moment. Poppy dropped the tassel and crossed her fingers. Cloud was the first to hear the distant sound of hooves coming from a nearby belt of trees, and his head shot up. Isadore, picking up on Cloud's unease, whinnied. The two horses were as still as stone as two masked highwaymen burst out of the trees and raced towards the picnic.

Beside the cameraman, Krystal gave a flick of her whip, her eyes on Cloud. The two bays were bearing down on the girls now, and Heidi's face was etched in fear as she clutched her on-screen sister in an Oscar-worthy performance.

The whip flicked again, and Cloud's head turned from the highwaymen to Krystal. Her hand was raised as if she were stopping traffic. Cloud didn't move a muscle.

The highwaymen were metres away now, and Krystal flicked the whip, giving Cloud the cue he'd been waiting for. *You can do it*, Poppy silently willed her pony. His head snapped up, and he pulled back from the stile, snapping the top rail in two. Krystal raised both arms in the air in the swooping movement Ned had used with Isadore. Cloud reared, once, twice, then a third time before he dropped to the ground and galloped off towards Claydon Manor, his reins flapping.

Poppy was about to spring to her feet and race after him when Ned stepped into his path and grabbed his reins. Giving Cloud a quick pat, he led him back up the track towards them.

Happy Cloud was safe, Poppy dragged her eyes from him to the highwaymen, who were busy demanding money with menaces from the picnicking sisters. Miss Jessie was shrieking while Miss Flora called to Isadore, 'Help us, Beauty! Please help us.'

Another flick of Krystal's wrist and Isadore broke free of the stile and trotted towards the highwaymen, his head twisting and his ears back. He stood on his back legs, waving his forelegs in the air. The highwaymen pulled their horses up, and Miss Flora scrambled to her feet. 'That's right, Beauty. You tell them!'

Isadore reared again and walked on his hindlegs towards the highwaymen, as he had with Ned in the indoor school. One of the horses pirouetted on the spot, and his rider dropped his pistol in surprise. Quick as a flash, Miss Flora scooped it up and trained it on him. 'Be on your way, or I'll shoot,' she cried, her finger on the trigger.

The older of the two highwaymen threw his head back and guffawed. 'Little miss says she's going to shoot us,' he crowed. 'I'll believe it when I see it.'

His accomplice sniggered.

And then three things happened at once. Krystal lifted her whip, Isadore charged at the riders, and Miss Flora pulled the trigger.

The gunshot was louder than Ned's cracking whip, and a couple of crows in a nearby beech tree soared into the sky, cawing shrilly. The older highwayman grasped his thigh and lifted his hand. It was crimson. His face twisted in anger.

'You shot me, you… you…'

'It's no more than you deserve, you heinous high-wayman. Now be gone from these parts. And believe me when I tell you that if you or your good-for-nothing friends ever show your faces here again, you'll have Beauty and me to answer to.'

Miss Flora raised the pistol again and took aim. As one, the two robbers turned tail and fled into the woods.

'Cut!' Kelvin cried as they disappeared from sight. Seconds later they reappeared, grinning and slapping each other on the back.

'That was so exciting,' Charlie said. 'I thought she'd really shot him.'

'Idiot!' Poppy biffed him on the shoulder. She wasn't about to admit that she'd thought so, too. Just for a second, anyway.

'Cloud was great, wasn't he?'

'He was really cool,' Charlie said. 'I'm going to ask the make-up girl how they make the fake blood. Won't be long.'

Poppy sat back and watched the goings-on through half-closed eyes. Ned had led Cloud and Isadore to a grassy area upstream, and the two horses were grazing side by side. Charlie was quizzing an earnest-looking man wearing cargo shorts, a baggy red teeshirt and a faded baseball hat. Heston and Kelvin were either side of the chief camera operator, watching the scene back. The actress playing Miss Jessie was having her make-up touched up. Something sharp in Heidi's backpack was digging into Poppy's thigh, and she lifted the bag onto the ground, yawned, and stretched out her legs.

As she made herself comfortable, she suppressed a smile. Heinous highwaymen indeed. Would Anna Sewell be turning in her grave, or would she be amazed that people still cared about her book nearly a hundred and fifty years later? Times weren't so different if you thought about it. It may have been highwaymen in the olden days, but thieves still thought it was OK to help themselves to other people's belongings.

Was PC Bodiam any closer to uncovering the identity of the purse thief? Now George Blackstone was out of the picture she must have had to start from scratch. Surely it had to be someone working on the set? So it was either a member of the crew, an extra or one of the actors. Poppy scanned the set, her gaze falling on Heidi, who was waiting to have her make-up re-touched.

Could Heidi be the culprit? She thought nothing of lying, that was for sure. She'd admitted pretending she could ride to get the part of Miss Flora. She also had cash to splash. Poppy pictured the platinum bangle, glinting in the sunshine. Like a magpie, Heidi was attracted to sparkly, shiny things. *And* she had the exact same phone as Scarlett. Too much of a coincidence?

Poppy wasn't about to accuse anyone without proof, not after the last time. She shifted position. As she did, her thigh brushed against Heidi's backpack.

What if she were to have a quick peek inside? If she couldn't find anything incriminating, no harm would be done. And if she did...

Poppy stole a furtive look at Heidi. She was sitting with her chin tilted up, and her eyes closed as the make-up girl brushed her cheeks with blusher. She'd be finished any minute. It was now or never.

Before she could change her mind, Poppy pulled open the drawstring top of the backpack and peered inside. The jumble of contents included hairbrushes, lipsticks, a small can of hairspray, a compact, a make-up bag, a Kindle with a hot pink case, a pair of sunglasses and the iPhone. Although Poppy knew it was face ID, she pressed the home button anyway. Scarlett's screensaver was a headshot of Red, taken the previous summer. Poppy had had to wave a bucket of nuts in front of him so his ears were pricked.

She took a deep breath and pressed the home button.

25

Sunflowers. A field of them. As yellow as mustard beneath a sky the colour of cobalt. In the background, a stone church. No chestnut geldings in sight. But that didn't mean anything. She could have swapped SIM cards and chosen her own photo as the screensaver. Poppy continued her search. Her hand closed around a large purse, and she pulled it out for a closer inspection. It was black leather with the familiar embossed Ted Baker lettering on the side, same as the backpack. Checking no-one was watching, Poppy opened the purse, finding various store cards, a couple of debit cards and sixty quid in cash inside. It was a lot of money for a teenage girl to be carrying around, but there was no way Poppy could prove it wasn't Heidi's. She closed the purse with a snap and dropped it back into the bag.

There was just the small zipped compartment left to check. Poppy gave the slider a tug and rootled around inside, all her focus on the contents. She pulled them out. A MAC lip gloss, Heidi's platinum bangle and a pair of matching earrings.

A shadow fell over her, and she jerked the zip shut and dropped the bag. 'How *do* you make fake blood?' she said, hiding her discomfiture behind a bright smile.

Ned frowned, and Poppy rubbed her eyes. 'Sorry, I thought you were my brother.'

'What were you doing?'

'Nothing.'

'That's Heidi Holland's bag. Why were you looking through it?'

'I wasn't.'

'Yes you were. I saw you.'

'Don't be ridiculous,' Poppy blustered, scrambling to her feet. 'Heidi asked me to look after it while they were filming. Anyway, where's Cloud? Aren't you doing another take?'

'He's with Krystal,' Ned said. 'And no, Heston's happy with the rushes. He doesn't need the horses again today.'

'They're having the afternoon off? Does that mean I can see Cloud?'

'I shouldn't think so, no.' An expression that Poppy couldn't read crossed Ned's face. He kicked the ground with his dusty riding boot. Her eye was drawn to a hoof-shaped dust mark on his black jodhpurs, just above his right knee.

'I saw you training Isadore earlier,' she began, but at that moment Charlie bowled over, his face alive with excitement.

'Golden syrup, cornflour, cocoa powder, red food colouring and water!' he said in a triumphant voice.

'*What?*'

'The ingredients you need to make fake blood. Joe, the special effects guy, told me. He has the coolest job in the world. Did you know, they use something called a squib to make the blood gush out when someone's shot? It's an exploding blood sack that's set off by a radio-controlled transmitter.'

Ned plunged his hands in his pockets and began walking away.

'Not now, Charlie,' Poppy muttered.

'The actor wears another little device on the belt of his trousers which is attached to the blood sack. When the transmitter's set off, it sends a signal to the blood sack which bursts, sending the fake blood everywhere.'

'Ned, wait,' Poppy called. But he either didn't hear or chose to ignore her. Poppy watched helplessly as he crossed the set to Krystal and took Cloud and Isadore from her.

'And you know the best thing?' Charlie continued. 'We've got all the ingredients at home, so I can make pints and pints of the stuff.'

———

THEY DECIDED to head home during the next break between scenes. Poppy had no desire to hang around the set all day if she couldn't see Cloud, and Charlie was itching to try his hand at making fake blood. As they went in search of their bikes, they bumped into a tall, blonde woman who dropped her black medicine bag on the floor when she saw them and pumped their hands. The last time they'd seen Sarah Brown, she was giving Cloud, Chester and Jenny their annual vaccinations just after Christmas.

'What are you doing here?' Poppy asked.

'I'm treating one of the stunt horses,' the vet said. 'A dappled grey Connie with a strained tendon. In fact, you'll never guess who he reminded me of?'

'Cloud,' the two children replied in unison.

'Oh. You've already seen him.'

'Cloud's playing Merrylegs while he's out of action,' Poppy explained.

'How exciting! Is that why you're here?'

She nodded. 'How is Perry?'

The vet picked up her bag and walked alongside them. 'So, so. The swelling's gone down, but he's still very lame. He's going to be on complete box rest for a while yet.'

'Poor thing.'

'Cloud's travelling up to Yorkshire with the rest of the horses on Monday, is he?' the vet asked.

It took a moment for her words to sink in. When they did, Poppy stopped in her tracks and stared at her open-mouthed. 'Yorkshire?'

'Krystal tells me they finish filming here this weekend, and they're off to Yorkshire on Monday to film the rest of the scenes on the North York Moors.'

'Cloud won't be going,' Poppy told her. 'He's coming home to Riverdale.'

'They have another lookalike, do they?'

'Yes.' *Did they?* Poppy realised her hands were balled into fists at her sides and her fingernails were pressing into her palms. She uncurled them and rubbed them on the front of her jeans.

'And I thought Cloud was a one-off.' The vet laughed, pointed her car keys at her filthy Land Rover and pressed the fob. There was an answering beep, and the hazard lights flashed. 'Best be off, or I'll be late for afternoon surgery. Nice to see you both. I'll look out for Cloud on the television.' She threw her bag into the boot, climbed into the driver's seat and roared off down the drive.

'Are you sure Cloud's not going to Yorkshire?' Charlie said, fixing the chinstrap of his helmet.

'Of course I'm sure,' Poppy growled. 'I'd never, ever let him travel so far from home.'

'That's all right then. The vet had me worried there for a minute.'

'I told you, there's nothing to worry about.' Poppy picked up her own helmet, then put it down again. 'Give me five minutes, will you? I, um, need the loo.'

Before Charlie had a chance to protest, Poppy jogged over to the Portaloos and, finding an empty one, held her nose and pushed open the door.

Once inside she pulled out her phone and scrolled through her emails until she found the one from Krystal King Stunt Horses. Opening it, she scanned the long letter. It was full of words like 'abovementioned', 'appertaining to' and 'indenture'. Frowning, she began to read.

This agreement is made on Saturday, April 3 between Poppy McKeever, who shall forthwith be referred to as the Owner, and Krystal King, who shall forthwith be referred to as the Trainer, and sets out the terms on which Cloud Nine is to be loaned by the Owner to the Trainer for the purposes of filming See Red's production of Black Beauty, which shall forthwith be referred to as the Production.

The agreement shall in no circumstances be interpreted or construed as an agreement for permanent transfer or any other purpose.

'I think that's good,' Poppy muttered.

It is agreed that at no time is the Trainer the registered owner of the Horse and as such is not permitted to loan, lease or sell the Horse to any third parties.

It all sounded correct and above board. The little knot in Poppy's stomach began to unfurl as she wondered what everyone was worried about. She read on.

The Trainer agrees to provide day to day care to the Horse and take all reasonable care to maintain the Horse in good condition at her own cost.

All good so far. But as Poppy scanned the next paragraph her brow furrowed and the knot in her belly tightened.

The loan shall commence on Saturday, April 3 and will

end when filming of the Production is complete. The Owner hereby gives her permission for the Horse to be transported at the Trainer's cost to any location used by See Red Productions for the filming of the Production as necessary.

Failure to comply will result in breach of contract, and the Trainer will be within her right to seek all costs and damages accrued.

Poppy grabbed hold of the sink as the words swam in front of her eyes. Did that mean Krystal could sue her if she didn't let her take Cloud to Yorkshire? Did Poppy even have a say in whether he went or not? She rubbed her face and stared at the contract. Her lips moved as she read it a second time. Then a third. But no matter how many times she pored over it, the meaning was clear. Krystal had every right to take Cloud to Yorkshire, and there was nothing she could do about it.

A sob caught in the back of her throat and she stared at the blue plastic ceiling and tried not to cry. The walls of the Portaloo closing in on her, she pushed the door open and staggered out, gulping lungfuls of fresh air.

Why hadn't she read the contract before she'd signed it? Or let Caroline or her dad see it? How naive she'd been. Of course Krystal needed Cloud for the rest of the filming. She didn't have time to find another Perry lookalike. She was a businesswoman with her own contract with See Red Productions to honour.

Poppy had thought it would be fun for Cloud to

step in as Merrylegs for a couple of weeks over the Easter holidays. After all, who wouldn't want their horse to star in a hit TV series? Poppy had missed him dreadfully, but knowing he was only a bike ride away had made their separation bearable. Plus the knowledge he'd be home by the end of the holidays.

Who knew how long the filming in Yorkshire would take? And what if there was another location after that? And another? Cloud could be away for weeks. Months, even. How would he cope, living so far from Riverdale and all the things he loved? Who would look after him if Poppy wasn't around?

Ned.

A chill struck deep in Poppy's chest at the thought. Ned, who saw nothing wrong in whipping a horse into compliance. Ned, who'd left Cloud in the horse walker, circling round and round like a caged hamster on a wheel. Ned, who was so slapdash he'd forgotten to give Cloud food and water, the basics needed to survive.

Poppy took a couple of shaky steps. Her legs felt feeble, as though she was recovering from a nasty bout of the flu. A sudden urge to see her stepmum overwhelmed her. Caroline would know what to do, she always did. Poppy took a deep breath, shoved her phone in her pocket and went in search of her brother.

oppy's spirits lifted a fraction when she saw a police car parked outside their house.

'Perhaps they've caught the thief,' she said, leaning her bike against the shed wall. 'I hope so, for Scarlett's sake.'

She followed Charlie around the side of the house and in through the back door.

'Poppy, is that you?' Caroline called. 'We're in the dining room.'

Poppy and Charlie looked at each other in surprise. Usually, the only time they used the dining room was for special occasions, like Christmas and Easter.

Charlie stuck his head around the dining room door.

'Oh, hi PC Bodiam. Have you caught the thief yet? Only if you haven't, I might be able to assist you in your inquiries.'

'Not now, Charlie. Go outside and play, please. PC Bodiam needs to have a little chat with Poppy.'

'But…' Charlie began.

'No buts, Charlie. Outside, now!' Caroline's voice was uncharacteristically curt, and Poppy's eyebrows shot up. Muttering under his breath, Charlie stalked past her to the back door. 'Poppy!' Caroline called again.

'I'm *coming*.' Dawdling down the hallway, she pushed the door open. PC Bodiam was sitting opposite Caroline, her pocket notebook open on the table in front of her. They both had glasses of water and wore serious expressions.

'Poppy, take a seat.' PC Bodiam indicated the chair next to Caroline. Poppy looked askance. Shouldn't they be inviting the police officer to sit down, not the other way around? It was their house, after all.

Hiding her confusion behind her fringe, she took a chair and looked sidelong at Caroline. Her stepmum's normally cheery demeanour was subdued, as if the sun had disappeared behind a cloud on a sunny summer's afternoon, and Poppy felt a resulting chill.

'Has something happened to Dad?' she blurted.

The question seemed to perplex both women. PC Bodiam flicked through her notebook, ending up on the same blank page she'd started on. Caroline shook her head and forced a laugh. 'No, Dad's fine. It's you PC Bodiam wanted to see.'

'Why, what's happened?'

PC Bodiam cleared her throat. 'We've received a phone call making a rather serious allegation I need to make you aware of.'

'Allegation?' Poppy thought of Ned nicking Isadore's ear with the lunge whip. But animal cruelty was a matter for the RSPCA, surely?

'But first I need to caution you…'

'Caution me?' Poppy echoed.

'You do not have to say anything. But it may harm your defence if you do not mention when questioned something which you later rely on in court. Anything you do say may be given in evidence.'

Poppy blinked. The only other times she'd heard those words was in television crime dramas. Caroline took her hand and gave it a squeeze. 'Don't worry,' she murmured. 'We'll sort this.'

But Poppy's eyes were glued to PC Bodiam's face. The officer picked up her notebook again. 'Someone rang the station earlier to report that they'd seen you with a handbag belonging to one of the actors on the set of Black Beauty. Is that true?'

'Well, yes. It was Heidi Holland's backpack. But I was looking after it for her.'

'She asked you to, did she?'

'Of course. I wouldn't have taken it otherwise.'

'According to the member of the public who rang in, you were rifling through the contents of Ms Holland's bag as though you were looking for something. Did she ask you to search the contents of her bag?'

Poppy felt first cold, then hot, as blood rushed up her neck to her cheeks. She pulled her hand from Caroline's grasp and rubbed her face. 'No, she didn't.'

'Why were you searching through her bag?'

Poppy was silent. PC Bodiam had warned her not to get involved after the fiasco at the Blackstone farm, and Poppy had promised she wouldn't. How could she now admit she'd changed her mind about Blackstone and thought Heidi was the thief and was trying to find evidence to prove it? The police officer would have every right to be furious. And Poppy couldn't even begin to imagine the look of disappointment on Caroline's face.

'Poppy?' Caroline said.

Poppy folded her arms across her chest and pursed her lips. 'I don't know.'

PC Bodiam laid her pen on the table and exhaled loudly. 'Help me understand, please, because from where I'm sitting it's not looking good. You were seen on the coach with Scarlett shortly before it was discovered that personal belongings, including phones and cash, had been stolen. You were caught on CCTV prowling around a local farm and entering the farmhouse without permission. And you were seen by an independent witness rifling through an actor's bag. The same actor who has since reported her designer bangle and matching earrings as stolen.'

Poppy gasped. 'I didn't take them, I promise.'

'Someone did. Until I have evidence to the contrary, I will be keeping an open mind.'

'You don't have any evidence it was me!'

'It's all circumstantial at this stage,' PC Bodiam admitted. 'But you see why I had no choice but to caution you. The guv'nor wants this all tied up before

Sniffer Smith and his ilk get even the faintest whiff of a scandal. If the story hits the papers, my head's on the block.' She smiled weakly. Neither Poppy nor Caroline smiled back.

'Who was your independent witness?' Poppy said.

'I'm not at liberty to disclose that information.'

'It was Ned from Krystal King Stunt Horses, wasn't it?'

'As I said, I'm not in a position to confirm or deny who called us.'

'What happens now?' Caroline asked.

'As Poppy can't tell me why she was searching through the bag I think we're done here for now. I'll be making further inquiries and will be in touch in due course about a second interview, which will be conducted back at the station.' The officer snapped her notebook shut and stood.

'I'll see you out,' Caroline said.

PC Bodiam gave a brief nod. At the door she paused and looked back at Poppy, who was slumped at the table with her head in her hands. 'I'm going now, Poppy. When you're ready to tell me what really happened, give me a call.'

———

CAROLINE FOUND Poppy at the edge of the paddock, gazing into the Riverdale wood. It was the same spot she'd first seen Cloud the day they'd moved to Riverdale and had seemed a fitting place to mourn his impending departure.

'Mind if I join you?'

Not waiting for an answer, Caroline sank onto the grass next to Poppy, so close their shoulders touched. Poppy leant against her.

'Claire's only doing her job.'

'I know. But you don't think I stole anything, do you?'

'Of course I don't. And Claire won't either when she's investigated further... Oh, don't cry, sweetheart. It's just a silly misunderstanding. It'll sort itself out, I promise.'

'It's not that,' Poppy sobbed. 'I couldn't care less about the stupid purse thief. It's Cloud. Krystal's taking him to Yorkshire on Monday for the rest of the filming. You're right, I should have read the contract, but I was too caught up in the glamour and excitement of it all to bother. She's within her rights to take him wherever she likes until filming has finished, and that could be months away. It's all here in black and white.' Poppy waved her phone at her stepmum.

'Let me see,' Caroline said. Her expression turned grim as she read the terms of the contract. 'You're fourteen. This Krystal woman should never have asked you to sign anything without either your dad or me present. It's unethical and may even be unlawful.'

Poppy sat up straight. 'You think so?'

Caroline smoothed Poppy's fringe away from her forehead. 'I do.'

'And Cloud won't have to go to Yorkshire?'

'Over my dead body,' Caroline said.

Poppy scrambled to her feet, suddenly energised. 'What are we going to do?'

Caroline held out a hand, and Poppy pulled her up. She dusted off her hands and placed them on her hips. 'We're going to see this Krystal woman so I can give her a piece of my mind.'

27

D oug the postman drove past in his van as they marched up to the house.

'Any post?' Caroline called to Charlie as she let herself in the back door.

'No!' came Charlie's muffled voice from upstairs.

Caroline frowned at Poppy. 'So why did Doug come to the house?'

'Force of habit?' said Poppy, who really couldn't care less. 'Can we go now?'

'Let me take Freddie out to stretch his legs.' Caroline checked her watch. 'Tell Charlie we're leaving in ten minutes.'

'Does he have to come?'

'I can't leave him here on his own.' Caroline whistled to Freddie, who was by her side in seconds, his feathery tail quivering with excitement.

Poppy bounded up the stairs to fetch a thicker jumper. She stopped outside Charlie's bedroom door. Usually, it was wedged open with his rocket-shaped door stop. Not today. She tried the handle and pushed, but the door was jammed shut. A voice squeaked, 'Who's that?'

'Only me,' she said, pushing harder. Suddenly the door flew open, propelling her forwards. 'What's going on?' she demanded.

Charlie glanced along the landing. Satisfied it was empty, he ushered her in and sat down with his back against the closed door. By his feet was a parcel wrapped in a grey plastic mailbag.

'What's that?' Poppy said. Her eyes narrowed. 'I thought you said there was no post?'

Charlie beckoned her closer. 'It's that stuff I was telling you about. The theft detection powder.' He attacked the bag with Caroline's nail scissors and pulled out a bundle of bubble wrap. Tearing it apart, his fingers closed around a small glass jar, half the size of a jam jar, with a black metal lid and a silver label.

'Visible stain thief detection powder,' Poppy read. 'For external use only. May cause staining.'

'May cause staining?' Charlie sniggered. 'I'd be pretty fed up if it didn't. It's kind of the point of it, after all.'

'How on earth did you get your sticky mitts on this? You're too young to have an eBay account.'

'Tory ordered it for me. I'm going to give her the money the next time she's over.'

'Does she know what it is?'

Charlie pulled a face. 'She thinks it's an extra ingredient for my chemistry set.'

Poppy shook her head. As she did her gaze fell on

their dad's old brown leather wallet on the rug next to Charlie. 'What's that doing here?'

Charlie opened the wallet, showing her two brand new ten-pound notes. 'It's the rest of my birthday money. I'm going to dust it with the powder and cycle over to Georgia's place before tea and plant it somewhere.'

'Charlie!' Poppy cried. 'I'm in enough trouble as it is without you playing detective, too.'

Charlie jutted his jaw. 'That's the point. I'm going to get you out of trouble. I heard everything PC Bodiam said.'

'How?'

'Does it matter?'

Poppy arched an eyebrow.

'OK, so I crept downstairs and listened at the door. I know you didn't steal anything and I'm going to prove it once and for all.'

'But...'

'The real thief's setting you up, can't you see? If we don't do something you'll be arrested and sent to jail, and the thief will get away with murder.' He paused. 'Not literally murder... at least I hope not.'

'I promised Mum and PC Bodiam I wouldn't get involved.'

Charlie gave her a crafty smile. 'You might have, but I didn't. I'm going to put the wallet in the pocket of one of Dad's old jackets which I'll leave on the back of a chair near the catering truck.'

Poppy noticed the cuff of an old corduroy jacket sticking out of Charlie's rucksack. 'I suppose no-one but the thief is going to rummage through someone else's pockets.'

'Exactly! I'm taking my camera so I can record everything. And these,' Charlie dangled a pair of Caroline's yellow washing up gloves in her face, 'are so I don't get the ink all over my hands. See? I've thought of everything.' His expression turned grave. 'You've got to trust me on this, sis. I know what I'm doing.'

'Do I have a choice?'

He shook his head.

'In that case, you'd better get ready. Mum's helping me get Cloud back from Krystal so you won't need to cycle over. We're leaving for Claydon Manor in five minutes.'

Charlie jumped to his feet, gathered his thief-catching kit and shoved it in his rucksack. Hitching it over one shoulder, he pulled his door open and grinned at his sister. 'I'll clear your name, don't you worry.'

Hitting her forehead with the palm of her hand, Poppy sighed loudly and followed him down the stairs.

'TELL me everything you know about this Krystal woman,' Caroline said as they set off for Claydon Manor. 'Forewarned is forearmed.'

'Um. She seems OK. It's her assistant, Ned, I'm not so sure about.'

'The one who came in the lorry to pick Cloud up?'

'That's him. He forgot to give Cloud hay and water

once, and yesterday he left him all alone in the horse walker. And I caught him whipping the horse playing Black Beauty. I couldn't bear it if he's been horrible to Cloud, too.'

Caroline tapped the steering wheel. 'It said something in the contract about the trainer having to provide day to day care and maintain Cloud in good condition. If she's broken her side of the contract it's null and void.'

'Good.' Poppy stared out of the window as Dartmoor's sage green tors and rocky outcrops whizzed past. Every now and then they passed a small herd of Dartmoor ponies, still fluffy in their winter coats. Behind her, Charlie was jiggling and fidgeting as if he had ants in his pants.

Caroline glanced at him in her rear-view mirror. 'Sit still, for goodness sake. We're nearly there.'

Soon they were turning into the Claydon drive. For once the gates were open, and Charlie waved at the CCTV camera as they drove through. Parking at the front of the house, Caroline jumped out and gazed around. 'It seems very quiet.'

'They must have finished filming for the day. Members of the cast are staying at local B&Bs and the crew are staying in the house. I bet Krystal and Ned are sleeping in the living areas of their horse lorries.'

'You'd better show me where they are.'

The lorries were parked on a small area of hardstanding behind the hay barn. They were both vast. Each big enough for at least five horses, Poppy guessed.

Plus generous living accommodation. Caroline reached up and rapped on the door of the nearest lorry.

Ned opened the door, holding a spoon in one hand and a tin of cold baked beans in the other. Poppy's stomach, already churning, roiled unpleasantly as she caught sight of the globular beans sitting in their gloopy sauce.

'I need to speak to Krystal King,' Caroline said.

Ned dipped the spoon in the tin, popped it into his mouth and chewed slowly. Poppy's stomach swirled again, and she breathed deeply and tried not to gag. Instead, she studied his body language. The way he lounged against the doorframe as he made Caroline wait yelled insolence, yet there was a wariness behind his eyes and a tiny tremor in his hands that he couldn't conceal.

Eventually, he finished chewing and pointed his empty spoon at the second lorry. 'She's in there.' Before Caroline could thank him, he'd disappeared inside and slammed the door.

'Which charm school did he go to?' Caroline said, shaking her head. 'Right, we'd better speak to Krystal.' She looked around. 'Where's Charlie?'

'He said something about needing the loo,' Poppy lied. How could she tell Caroline the truth - that he'd slipped away to plant his trap? Crossing her fingers behind her back, she followed Caroline to the second lorry.

'Come in,' Krystal called, in answer to Caroline's knock. Giving Poppy a reassuring smile, Caroline pulled open the door.

The horse master was sitting on the bench seat that ran along the back wall of the lorry's living accommodation. Her folded wheelchair was sandwiched between the end of the seat and the wall. Seeing Poppy's eyes slide over it, Krystal said, 'I do have limited mobility. I can just about manage without my chair in here if I hold onto the counters for support.'

Poppy blinked. She'd assumed Krystal was completely paralysed from the waist down. Hadn't she said as much, the first time they'd met? Poppy cast her mind back, but although she could remember the gist of the conversation, she couldn't remember Krystal's exact words. Perhaps she'd jumped to conclusions. She fished around for something to say, ending up with a lame, 'That's good.'

'Please, take a seat. What can I do for you?'

Caroline perched on the edge of the seat, her hands between her knees. 'We're a little concerned about you taking Cloud to Yorkshire for the rest of the filming.'

'I see.'

Caroline took a deep breath. 'My husband and I are also concerned that you thought it was appropriate for Poppy to sign the contract without either of us present.'

'Where is he? Your husband?'

'In London, why?'

'He can't be that concerned then, can he?'

Caroline frowned. 'The thing is, we think you're going to have to find another pony to play Merrylegs.'

'Find another pony to play Merrylegs, just like that, eh?' Krystal's voice was caustic. 'Have you any idea how hard it is to find identical ponies, especially at such short notice? I'll tell you, shall I? Virtually impossible.'

'But if Poppy had thought there was even the slightest chance that you were planning to take him out of the county she'd never have agreed to you having him.'

Poppy nodded. 'That's right.'

Krystal tapped her fingernails on the arm of the seat and then pointed at Poppy. 'It was there in the contract in black and white, and she signed it.'

'She's fourteen. She doesn't understand legal terminology.' A flush had crept up Caroline's neck. 'Perhaps I'm not making myself clear. We feel Poppy signed the contract under duress and as such it's null and void.'

'Under duress? I've heard it all now.' Krystal threw her head back and laughed. Poppy couldn't tear her eyes away from the horse master's protruding neck muscles. 'She was happy enough for me to take him when she saw how much money she was getting.'

'That's not true!' Poppy cried.

'Then why did you sign over your precious pony to me?'

'Because I wanted to help you out. Because I thought he'd enjoy it. Because…'

'Because you thought it would be fun to be the owner of Merrylegs off the telly.'

Poppy flinched. Krystal smirked. 'I thought so.'

'This isn't getting us anywhere,' Caroline said, standing. 'You'll get your money back. You have my word. And we'll be sending a trailer over in the morning to collect Cloud. Come on, Poppy, let's go.'

As Poppy joined her stepmum by the door, Krystal said, 'Wait!'

Caroline turned, her hand grasping the doorframe.

'They're shooting Merrylegs' last scene here tomorrow night. Let me use him for that, then you can have him back, and I'll find another pony for Yorkshire.'

Caroline glanced at Poppy. 'What d'you think?'

Poppy chewed her bottom lip.

'Otherwise, I'll have no choice but to use Perry,' Krystal said.

'But Perry's lame!' Poppy cried.

The horse master shrugged. 'It won't be the first time I've had to use an injured horse during filming, and I dare say it won't be the last. Needs must.'

Poppy shook her head in disbelief. She couldn't bring herself to look at Krystal. Instead, she muttered to Caroline, 'OK, she can have him for one last night. Then we're bringing him home.'

P oppy almost collided with Charlie as she jumped down from the lorry.

'Where's Mum?' he hissed, pulling her around to the front of the cab.

'Inside. Did you do it?'

He nodded. His eyes gleamed. 'The trap is set. I left Dad's jacket by the catering truck. I came back past the stables so I could say hello to Cloud. And I found this in his stable.'

He pulled something out of his rucksack and handed it to Poppy. It was a length of black plastic with a loop of rope sticking out of one end.

Poppy twisted it in her hands and pulled on the rope. It didn't move a millimetre. 'What is it?'

'I don't know,' Charlie admitted. 'But I thought you ought to see it.'

'There you are,' Caroline said, making them both jump. 'We're done here. Let's go home.'

'Can I give this to Cloud?' Poppy said, shoving the

stick into the waistband of her jeans and producing a carrot from her pocket.

'If you're quick. We'll see you by the car.'

Poppy sped towards the stable block, not caring if Krystal or Ned saw her. The horse master had shown her true colours this evening. There was no getting away from it, she didn't care about her horses. To her, they were simply a means to an end. Working animals who were treated not with compassion but as commodities.

Brian whickered as she jogged past his stable, and she paused to scratch his nose. Smelling the carrot, the big bay gelding nudged her, and she snapped it in two and offered him half.

Once again, Cloud was standing at the back of his stable. His ears were pricked, and his eyes never left hers as she slid open the bolt and let herself in. She gave him the rest of the carrot and flung her arms around his neck, burying her face in his coat and drinking in his familiar smell.

'I'm so sorry, Cloud. I should never have let you come here. But you're almost done. One more day and you'll be home.'

Stepping back, she reached up to scratch the soft area behind his ear, something that usually sent him into a blissful stupor. But he jerked his head away, bashing her square on the nose.

'Ow!' Her hand flew to her face, and her eyes sprang with tears. She shook her head until the pain passed, then inspected her hand, wincing when she saw a smear of blood. Cloud watched warily as she wiped her nose on her sleeve.

'It's all right, silly,' she said. 'I'm not cross with you. It was an accident. You didn't mean it. But you normally love having your ear scratched.' She approached him again, more slowly this time, and stroked his nose. 'You've never been head shy before. Did Ned do something to you?' Rubbing his cheek, she gazed into his eyes. 'I wish you could tell me what's wrong.'

The stick was digging into her stomach and, without thinking, she pulled it out. The reaction from Cloud was instant. He threw his head up and whirled around, pressing himself into the farthest corner of the stable. His ears flicked back and forth, his gaze on the length of plastic.

Feeling as though a hole had opened up beneath her feet and she was tumbling through it, Poppy drew back. Her heart was racing. Why was Cloud so terrified of the stick? What had it been used for? Talking to him in a low, steady voice, she backed towards the door and dropped it outside. Cloud flinched as it clattered onto the concrete. Showing him her hands were empty, she inched her way towards him.

'It's OK, Cloud. You know I'd never hurt you.'

Tentatively, he nuzzled her hair. Poppy ran a hand along his neck and wished with all her heart that she'd never agreed to let him go.

THEY DROVE HOME IN SILENCE, each lost in their own thoughts. As Caroline turned into their lane, Poppy's hand was on the seatbelt buckle.

'Can you drop me at Ashworthy? I want to see Scarlett.'

'As long as you're back for tea,' Caroline said, pulling into the farm's potholed drive.

Poppy smiled her thanks and jumped out of the car. She found Scarlett making a half-hearted attempt to square off her muckheap.

'Need any help?' Poppy said, picking up a spare fork.

Scarlett brushed her fringe away from her eyes with the back of her rubber-gloved hand. 'I wouldn't say no.' She looked at Poppy closely. 'You look like someone just cancelled Christmas. What's wrong?'

As they worked side by side forking the dirty straw, Poppy described their trip to Claydon Manor, Caroline's showdown with Krystal and Cloud's reaction to the plastic stick.

'D'you have it with you?'

'I left it in the car. But it was about half a metre long and had a loop of rope attached to one end.'

'That sounds like a twitch.'

'A what?'

'Vets sometimes use them to restrain horses if they're giving them an injection or something.'

'How do they work?'

Scarlett pulled a face. 'They loop the rope bit over a horse's top lip and twist the stick until the rope's tight.

It's supposed to stop the horse thrashing about. Some people use it on a horse's ears.'

'That's inhumane!' Poppy cried.

'Do you think Ned's used it on Cloud?'

'He must have. Charlie found it in his stable, and Cloud was terrified when he saw it.' Her face drained of colour. 'Oh Scarlett, I've been so stupid. I should never have let Krystal have Cloud.'

Scarlett left her fork in the muckheap and put a shoulder around Poppy. 'I feel bad that I talked you into it.'

A tear trickled down Poppy's cheek. 'I would have agreed anyway. I liked the idea of having a famous pony.' She sniffed. 'I was even going to set him up his own Instagram account to see if he could become a brand ambassador, too.'

'And there I was, worrying you thought *I* was shallow.'

'I know. Turns out I'm just as bad as you. Actually worse, because I was happy to hand my pony over for fame and fortune.'

'Don't be too hard on yourself. You were helping Krystal out, too. She did a pretty good job of guilting you into it, I seem to remember.'

'She told me she'd have to bute Perry up to his eyeballs if I didn't lend her Cloud.'

'Exactly!'

'And I thought she was cool. I wanted to impress her.' There, she'd said it.

'She manipulated you. Simple as. Don't beat your-self up about it.'

Poppy smiled weakly and leant on the handle of her fork. 'But that's only the half of it. I'm about to be arrested for stealing your phone and my own money.'

'What?'

Poppy recounted PC Bodiam's visit and the impending interview at Tavistock Police Station.

'I don't understand why you thought Heidi was the thief,' Scarlett said.

'Because she was waving her expensive bangle about and she has exactly the same phone as you.'

'About eleven-billion other people in the world have the same phone as me. And of course she's loaded. She's a famous actress!'

Not that famous, Poppy was about to say but stopped herself just in time. She was already in trouble with Scarlett for judging people. Instead, she said, 'Anyway, we'll soon know who the thief is. Charlie's set a trap.'

Scarlett's eyes grew wider as Poppy told her about the thief detection powder.

'What happens now?'

'Charlie and I need an excuse to visit the set tomorrow. Krystal said they were shooting a night scene.'

'But they've finished with the extras. Heidi told me.'

Poppy rubbed the back of her neck. 'I was wondering if you could call Heidi to see if we can get permission to watch? That way, Charlie can look out for the thief, and I can keep an eye on Cloud.'

Scarlett gave Poppy an appraising look. 'You're happy to accuse her of being a thief until you need her help.'

Poppy held her hands up. 'It's hypocritical, I know. But I've changed my ways, I promise.'

Scarlett rolled her eyes. 'I'll believe it when I see it.' She chewed her bottom lip. 'All right, I'll do it. On one condition.'

'Anything.'

'That I can come, too. I'm not missing this for the world.'

29

Scarlett phoned Poppy later that evening to tell her everything had been arranged.

'Heidi's cleared it with Kelvin. I told her to tell him we're both thinking about choosing film studies for A-level.'

'And he believed her?'

'Of course he believed her. She's an actress, remember.'

'Cool. I'll tell Caroline we're going to yours for tea, and you tell your mum you're having tea at ours, and we'll meet at the bottom of the drive at six. Which scene are they filming, by the way?'

'The one where Miss Flora has to ride Merrylegs through the night to fetch the doctor because her mum's gravely ill.'

Poppy's heart gave a little leap. 'I hope Cloud will be OK.'

'Heidi said she's having a couple of one-to-one lessons with Krystal before and after lunch.'

Rather than succumbing to her usual flare-up of jealousy, Poppy was glad Cloud was spending his last day at Claydon Manor with someone who doted on him. 'Good,' she said, smiling down the phone. And then something occurred to her. 'Wasn't it Black Beauty and John Manly who went for help when Mrs Gordon was ill?'

Scarlett laughed. 'It's that artistic licence again. Let's face it, this show is nothing like Anna Sewell's book.'

CHARLIE CAME into Poppy's room at a quarter to six the following evening. He sat on the end of her bed with his rucksack on his knees.

'Have you got everything?' she asked him. 'Camera?'

'Check.'

'Bike lights?'

'Check.'

'Head torches?'

He tapped the rucksack.

'And I've got my phone.' Poppy grabbed her coat from the back of the door. 'C'mon, let's go catch a thief.'

She poked her head around the lounge door. Caroline was watching a repeat of Come Dine With Me, her guilty pleasure. 'We're going. We'll be back about half eight.'

'Kind of Pat to invite Charlie, too. I must remember to phone her in the morning to thank her.'

Poppy gripped the door handle. 'No need. I'll tell her tonight.'

'Make sure you do. Have a nice time.'

Sagging against the door, Poppy said hoarsely, 'We will.' She was letting herself out of the back door when Caroline called, 'Poppy, wait a minute!'

She froze, a fake smile plastered to her face. 'What is it?'

Her stepmum appeared in the kitchen holding a cookbook. 'Pat wanted my recipe for coffee and walnut cake. Tell her she can borrow the book as long as she wants.'

'Sure.'

Her stepmum peered out of the window. 'Why's Charlie on his bike? You're only going next door.'

'We thought it'd be quicker to cycle.'

Caroline's eyes narrowed. 'You wouldn't…' She gave a little shake of her head. 'Of course you wouldn't. You gave me your word.' She gave Poppy the cookbook. 'I'll see you later.'

Poppy ran a hand across her brow as she joined Charlie outside. 'Phew, that was close. For a minute I thought Mum had guessed we were up to something.'

Charlie grinned. 'Can you blame her? We usually are.'

———

SCARLETT HID the cookbook in a bush at the bottom of the Ashworthy drive, and they pedalled to Claydon Manor discussing their plan of action.

'First, we'll see if Dad's jacket and the wallet are still there,' Charlie said. 'If the wallet's gone, we need to check everyone's hands.'

'What are we looking for?' Scarlett asked.

'Someone with a dark purple stain on their fingers,' Charlie said.

'They could be wearing gloves,' Poppy pointed out. 'What do we do then?'

'Pretend your hands are cold and ask to borrow them. If they say no, there's a pretty good chance we've found our man.'

'Or woman,' Scarlett said. 'What do we do when we find them?'

Poppy, who hadn't thought much beyond catching the culprit, shrugged. 'Call the police, I guess. But I'm checking Cloud's OK first. Scar, can you stick close to Charlie to make sure he's OK?'

'I don't need nannying,' Charlie spluttered.

Scarlett said, 'You might not, but I do. Will you stick close to me?'

''Course I will,' he said, stamping down on his pedals and shooting forwards.

'Thanks,' Poppy mouthed to Scarlett.

'No problem,' she whispered back.

Reaching Claydon's wrought iron gates, Poppy pressed the buzzer.

'Yes?' came a tinny reply.

'We're here to see Georgia. She's expecting us.' Poppy waved at the CCTV camera on top of the nearest gate post and, with a creak, the gates swung open.

Scarlett cocked an eyebrow.

'I texted her to say we might pop by,' Poppy said. 'I had to, didn't I? Otherwise, they might not have let us in.'

When they reached the house, they abandoned the bikes and split up. Scarlett and Charlie headed for the catering truck to see if the jacket was still there, and Poppy made her way to the stables. As she passed the runner, who was chatting up one of the make-up girls, she found herself peeking at their hands, looking for traces of purple ink. Nothing.

Poppy plunged her own hands into her pockets. Were they insane to think Charlie's plan might actually work? PC Bodiam would have a meltdown if she knew they were once again meddling in her investigation. And Poppy hated lying to Caroline. But the worst-case scenario, she reasoned, was that the thief was too smart to fall for their trick, in which case they could leave it to the police knowing they'd at least tried. The best-case scenario was that they caught the thief and proved her innocence once and for all.

She stopped outside Cloud's stable, and his head appeared over the door before she had a chance to call him. Ned must have been busy. Heß was immaculate, his dappled grey coat as sleek and lustrous as molten silver. Wondering yet again how Ned did it - Shine spray? Blue shampoo? Magic? - she let herself into the stable.

'Hey baby,' she crooned, running her hand along Cloud's silky flank. 'One more sleep and you'll be home.' Her gaze fell on the hay rack. Empty. She crossed the stable to the water feeder. Bone dry. Cloud barged past her, his lips nuzzling the empty bowl. Something inside Poppy snapped.

'The lazy toad. How could he leave you without hay and water *again*?' She ran her hand through her hair. 'Well, he's going to wish he hadn't by the time I've finished with him.' She turned on the drinker and water spurted out. Leaving Cloud slurping greedily, she marched out of the stable in search of Ned, blood pounding in her ears.

———

SHE FOUND him in the back of one of the horse lorries, fiddling with the partitions.

'How *dare* you leave Cloud with no hay or water *again*?'

He turned slowly, stuffing his hands in his pockets. 'It's none of your business what I do or don't do.'

'Of *course* it's my business. He's my pony!' Poppy cried.

'He's Krystal's until the end of the shoot. You signed a contract, remember.'

'And as part of that contract, Krystal promised to take good care of him. And letting him go hungry and thirsty is NOT TAKING GOOD CARE OF HIM!' Poppy stepped forwards until her face was centimetres from Ned's. 'I'd say she'd broken her side of the contract, wouldn't you?' She looked him up and down, her attention caught by a mark on his buff-coloured jodhpurs. She held his gaze for a moment, then spun on her heels and pulled her phone from her pocket.

'What are you doing?'

'Phoning the RSPCA and reporting you for animal cruelty.'

Ned surged forwards. His hand shot out of his pocket, and he lunged for the phone. But Poppy was too quick. She darted out of his reach and stared him down, her finger poised over the keypad.

'Or should I phone 999 to report you for theft?' she said, staring at his right hand, which was stained purple from the inside of his wrist to the tips of his fingers. It looked like a particularly colourful bruise.

'I can explain everything…' Ned stammered.

Poppy laughed without mirth. 'Now this I have to hear.'

He stole a glance over his shoulder. 'Not here. In the horse lorry.'

Without stopping to consider whether or not it was a good idea, Poppy followed him into the living accommodation, the door swinging closed behind her.

30

Ned slumped on the bench seat with his head in his hands. On the draining board sat a nail brush and a bar of purple-stained soap. He lifted his head, held out his palms and stared at her bleakly.

'What the hell is this stuff?'

'Thief detection powder. It stains when it comes into contact with someone's skin. We set a trap to catch a thief, and it looks as though it worked like a dream.'

'You left the wallet in that jacket?'

'Not me. My brother, Charlie. He wanted to prove my innocence. Because the police think I'm the one who's been stealing things, you see.' Poppy stared at him, a memory resurfacing. 'You saw me looking through Heidi's bag. I bet you're the one who rang the police station.'

Ned lowered his gaze, and Poppy knew she was right.

'How could you?'

'I wasn't lying. You were looking through Heidi's things,' he said.

'Not because I was looking for something to steal! I thought *she* was the thief. Looks like I was wrong again. It was you all along.'

'You don't understand...'

'Oh, I understand all right. You've been helping yourself to other people's stuff since the first day of filming. Working with the horses made you invisible to the cast and crew. Neat. And then you decided to set *me* up!' She tightened her grip on her phone. 'You said you could explain everything. Go on then, I'm all ears.'

Ned stared at his hands. 'You're right. I did steal your friend's phone, your money and Heidi Holland's jewellery. But I needed the money. I mean, *really* needed it.'

'Why?'

'I need to get away from Krystal. I can't do this job any longer.' His shoulders sagged. 'But she pays me minimum wage then charges me rent and by the time I've paid that there's nothing left. I don't even have enough money for a train ticket out of here. I'm stuck with her.'

'Why do you want to leave?'

His eyes blazed. 'You don't get it, do you?'

'Get what? It's a dream job. I'd love to work with horses.'

'And I love working with them, too. It's Krystal that's the problem.' His Adam's apple bobbed up and down as he swallowed. 'She's evil.'

Poppy wrinkled her nose. 'Evil?'

'You think I like leaving a pony with no hay or water? You think I like using a whip on a horse?' He gave a muffled noise, somewhere between a groan and a sob. 'She makes me. I'm just following orders.'

'Right, of course. How convenient. You're following orders. And did Krystal tell you to steal Scarlett's phone and my money, too?' Poppy scoffed.

Ned slammed his hand on his thigh and Poppy shrank back.

'That's not what I said. I told you, I need the money if I'm going to make a break for it.'

Make a break for it? The way Ned was talking, you'd think he was planning to escape from prison, not leaving a job he no longer wanted.

'Why d'you think she told me to leave your pony without any hay or water?'

'She said you were sloppy.'

He gave a hollow laugh. 'I follow her orders to the letter. It's not worth the grief not to. She told me to turn off his water and take away his hay.'

'But why?'

'You don't know anything, do you? Taking away food and water from highly-strung horses keeps them placid. It's an old trick dealers used to use to make people think they were buying a calm horse. Some dealers probably still do. After that pony of yours kicked off during filming the other day, Krystal decided she couldn't risk it happening again. She told me to take his food and water away the night before every scene.'

'But…'

'That's why he was in the horse walker yesterday. Krystal wanted me to wear him out before filming.'

Poppy's mind whirled. 'She made you use the whip on Isadore, too, did she?'

'Krystal's probably told you about her "unique" training methods,' Ned said, drawing imaginary apostrophes in the air with his purple-stained fingers. 'Let's just say she prefers the stick to the carrot.' He opened his arms wide. 'Natural horsemanship this ain't.'

'But I've never once seen Krystal do anything cruel to any of the horses. How do I know you're telling the truth?'

Ned reached into his pocket and pulled out his phone. It was an old model, even older than Poppy's, and had a large crack across the screen. As if reading her mind, he said, 'I'm not bothered by shiny new things. I told you, I need the money to get away.' He tapped in his passcode, opened his photos and handed the phone to Poppy. 'Watch this and then tell me you don't believe me.'

Poppy stared at the screen. A palomino horse stood in the centre of a small, covered enclosure. Shafts of sunlight streamed in, crisscrossing his coat like the stripes of a zebra. The horse was still, his head unnaturally high. Poppy used her fingers to zoom in. Her gaze was drawn to the whites of his eyes and then to his nostrils, as flared as trumpets. And then she saw something that made the hairs on the back of her neck stand up. His headcollar was hooked to a chain hanging from a rafter. The horse stiffened as Krystal's wheelchair came into view. She crossed the enclosure to a winch in the wall and turned the handle. As she did the chain creaked, and the horse's head jerked up.

Poppy turned away and flung the phone in Ned's direction.

'They're left like that overnight with no food or water. When it's time to train them, they never put up a fight.'

'It's… brutal,' Poppy whispered.

'She's always telling me I'm too soft because I don't tie the horses up tight enough. Once she caught me taking a bucket of water to Isadore in the middle of the night. She docked me a week's wages. God knows what she'd do if she knew I'd filmed her.'

A thought occurred to Poppy that was so horrific she could barely muster up the courage to ask. 'Did she… did she do this to Cloud?'

Ned shook his head. 'Her reputation as a famous trainer is far too precious to her to risk that. Imagine if someone found out the legendary Krystal King abused her horses to get results? She only uses the chain at her yard.'

'But she used a twitch on him?'

'Probably. She uses a twitch on them all.'

Poppy's throat burned. The atmosphere was oppressive, and the urge to leave was overwhelming. She pulled open the door and was about to jump out when Ned grabbed her arm.

'Wait!'

Poppy wriggled out of his grip. 'Get your hands off me!'

'Sorry,' he said, shrinking back as if she'd slapped him. His face crumpled. 'I need to know what you're going to do.'

'I'm taking Cloud home, that's what I'm going to do. And the minute he is home, I'm calling the police.'

'You're going to tell them about me?'

'Of course I am.'

'It's all here, the stuff I stole.' Ned opened a cupboard under the bench seat and pulled out a plastic carrier bag. He went to hand it to Poppy.

'D'you think I'm stupid? I'm not leaving my finger-prints all over that.'

'That's not what I meant for you to do, honest.'

'Honest?' Poppy jeered. 'That's rich, coming from you.'

Ned continued as if she hadn't spoken. 'I wanted to show you that I still have everything and I'll give it all back if you promise not to tell the police.'

Poppy shook her head. 'I don't have time for this. I need to see Cloud.'

Ned glanced at his watch. 'You're too late. They're due to start filming in fifteen minutes. Krystal will have taken him onto the moor by now.'

'Why didn't you take him?'

'I was supposed to be getting the lorry ready.' Ned turned abruptly and stared out of the window into the night.

Poppy's insides turned to ice. 'Ready for what?'

31

Ned opened his mouth, then closed it again. He blew his cheeks out, then released the air with a loud puff.

'Ned?'

'Krystal's planning something.'

'What?'

'I'll tell you if you promise not to call the police.'

'I can't...'

'It's about your pony.'

'How do I know you're not bluffing?'

'Was I bluffing about the abuse?'

Poppy shook her head.

'Well?'

She was silent. What mattered most - exposing a thief or keeping Cloud safe? But... maybe there was another way.

'If you give me the things you stole I'll make sure they're returned to their rightful owners.'

'And you won't call the old bill?'

'Not if you tell me what Krystal's planning.'

Ned picked up the carrier bag and twisted it in his hands. 'We're leaving with the horses tonight, the minute filming is finished.' He looked meaningfully at her. '*All* of the horses.'

Poppy blinked. 'Including Cloud?'

He nodded. 'Krystal's spent the last twenty-four hours phoning around all her contacts in the horse world, but no-one has a pony that looks anything like Perry. And she can't risk using him. She knows that if there's the faintest chance someone notices he's lame the animal rights brigade will be onto the production company like a ton of bricks. She needs Cloud in Yorkshire.'

'But he's not hers to take.'

'She'll give him back once she's finished with him.'

Once she's finished with him. Poppy blanched. 'Will you help me rescue him?'

Ned shook his head. 'Sorry, I'm outta here. There's no way I'm hanging around to find out what happens when Krystal realises I've betrayed her.'

Thinking quickly, Poppy said, 'AirDrop me that film.' Ned bent over his phone, and a moment later her phone pinged. She accepted the footage and picked up the carrier bag. 'I'll tell Kelvin I found it behind the Portaloos.'

'Thanks.' Ned began ramming clothes into a worn rucksack. When it was full, he fixed the straps and hefted it onto his back. 'There is one way you could take Cloud without Krystal becoming suspicious.'

'Tell me,' Poppy demanded.

'You won't be able to do it on your own. You'll need Heidi Holland's help.'

AS POPPY JOGGED towards the manor house, the handle of the carrier bag wrapped around her wrist, her phone chirruped with a text from Scarlett.

We've been looking for you everywhere. Where ARE you??

Just coming. Where are you? Poppy typed back.

On set. They're having their last run-through before filming starts. We still haven't seen any purple hands, have you?

Tell you when I see you. Is Cloud there?

He's with Krystal, Scarlett confirmed. *Tell me NOW!!*

No time. I'll be with you in a couple of minutes. Oh, and grab Heidi, will you? I need to speak to her NOW.

Curiouser and curiouser, Scarlett typed back. *I'll see what I can do.*

Poppy quickened her pace until she was running. Reaching the back of the house, she stopped, her hands on her knees as she caught her breath. Kelvin was standing in front of three huge spotlights trained on the ornate front door.

'Good job, people. We'll take a quick break before the first take. Back here in ten minutes.'

Poppy made a beeline for him.

'Excuse me, Kelvin?' she said, stepping in front of him.

He frowned. 'What are you doing here? We don't

need any extras tonight.'

'Heidi said it would be OK if we watched.'

His face cleared. 'Oh yes, you're one of the girls who wants to do film studies. Let me guess, you'd like to quiz me about my long and illustrious career in television?'

'Um, I'd love to, but I don't have time at the moment. I just wanted to give you this. I found it behind the Portaloos.'

Poppy handed Kelvin the carrier bag. He opened it up and stared inside.

'I think it's all the stuff that's been stolen over the past couple of weeks,' Poppy said.

'Well I never.'

'Perhaps whoever took it had a pang of conscience, or decided it was too hot to handle. Will you call the police to tell them?'

Kelvin nodded. 'We're on a break. I'll ring them now.'

Spying Scarlett and Charlie sitting cross-legged on the grass, Poppy darted over to join them.

'Before you say anything, I don't have time to tell you everything now. I need to speak to Heidi. Where is she?'

'In make-up,' Scarlett said. 'She's coming over when she's done.'

'Great, thanks.' Shielding her eyes from the glare of the spotlights, Poppy peered at Heidi. Dressed in a dark-grey hooded cloak, the young actress was having her face powdered by one of the make-up girls. 'Is that what she's wearing for the next scene?'

Scarlett nodded.

'Tell me what happens, from the minute the scene opens.'

'First Heidi looks out of that window,' Scarlett said, pointing to the nearest sash window on the first floor of the manor house. 'Then the front door bursts open and she comes running out to John Manly, who's holding Merrylegs outside. He gives her a leg-up and wishes her a safe journey, and she gallops off into the night.'

'Which way does she gallop, along the drive or around the back of the house towards the moor?'

'Towards the moor,' Scarlett said.

'Cool. Where's Cloud?'

'Over there,' Charlie said. Poppy followed his gaze. Cloud was standing by Krystal's wheelchair as she chatted to the actor playing Squire Gordon's head groom. Poppy's heart contracted with love for her pony. Would Ned's idea work? It was risky, that was for sure. Audacious, even. Was she mad to even consider it? But the clock was ticking. There wasn't time to argue about broken contracts or attempt to reason with Krystal. Poppy had to play her at her own game. Play her… and win.

'Here comes Heidi,' Scarlett said. She patted the ground, and Heidi sat next to her.

'So,' she said, her eyes shining. 'What's the big secret?'

Poppy beckoned them closer, and one by one, their mouths dropped open as she shared Ned's crazy plan.

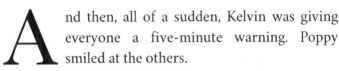

nd then, all of a sudden, Kelvin was giving everyone a five-minute warning. Poppy smiled at the others.

'It's time. Everyone ready?'

Scarlett and Charlie nodded, but Poppy only saw their bobbing heads in her peripheral vision. Her eyes hadn't left Heidi's face. The actress had listened in silence as Poppy had outlined the plan, and hadn't said a word since. Scarlett and Charlie were used to her harebrained schemes, but this was all new to Heidi and Poppy had no idea what was going through her mind. Yet their plan depended on her. If she got cold feet, they had a major problem. 'Heidi?' Poppy said. 'Are you with us?'

Heidi dipped her head. 'One hundred per cent.' She scrambled to her feet. 'What are we waiting for?'

Poppy stood in the shadows, her head cocked to one side as she listened to Heston running through his last-minute checks. She'd heard them so many times over the last couple of weeks that she knew them off by heart. Her lips moved as she reeled them off in her head. *Everyone at their stations. Quiet on set! Roll sound. Roll camera.* Then Kelvin's voice. 'Scene thirty-eight, take one.' The sharp crack of the clapperboard and an answering, 'Set!' from the cameraman.

'Good luck,' Poppy whispered to Heidi, standing a few feet away. 'And thank you.'

Heidi glanced at Poppy and smiled. As Poppy shrank back into the shadows, she heard the sound of hooves on gravel. She crossed her fingers and stared at the ceiling, sending a plea skywards. *Please let this crazy plan of ours work. For Cloud's sake.*

She pictured Heston raising the megaphone to his lips. His voice sounded muffled from behind the heavy damask curtains she was hiding behind. 'And... action!' he cried.

Heidi stepped in front of the window, her hands shielding her eyes as she stared through the glass. After what seemed like an age, while Poppy's heart crashed wildly in her chest, Heston yelled, 'Cut!' and then, 'Next scene, please.'

'He's on a mission tonight,' Heidi said, joining Poppy behind the curtains. 'He usually makes me do at least a couple of takes.'

'Which means we don't have long.' Poppy took the cape from Heidi and shrugged it over her shoulders.

Her fingers were trembling as she tried to fix the fastenings.

'Let me do them,' Heidi said. 'You know what to do, right? Let yourself out of the door, making sure your head's down and the hood's covering your face. On the doorstep stop and look back over each shoulder like I showed you. And then tiptoe across the gravel towards John Manly and Cloud. Keep your head down. Hopefully, he won't realise you're not me until after he's given you a leg up. Then you swing Cloud around and gallop off towards the moor. We were supposed to stop by the gateway and walk back to the set.'

'But we need to keep going,' Poppy said. 'So when it all kicks off…'

'Just show Heston or Kelvin Ned's footage.' Heidi's face was grim. 'As soon as they realise what Krystal's been up to you'll be off the hook.'

Both girls froze as a voice carried up the stairs.

'Ready Heidi?' Heston called.

Heidi cocked an eyebrow at Poppy. 'Ready?' she whispered.

Feeling as though she was standing on the edge of danger, but knowing she had no choice but to take the plunge, Poppy nodded, pulled the hood over her head and crossed to the top of Claydon's sweeping wooden staircase.

'Ready!' Heidi yelled.

'Scene thirty-nine, take one.'

'And… action!'

AFTERWARDS, Poppy wondered how she'd held her nerve. Her legs had felt like jelly as she'd walked downstairs, across the wide hall and out of the front door. Careful to make sure her face was hidden, she'd glanced back, just as Heidi had shown her, then crept across the gravel towards Cloud and the actor playing Squire Gordon's groom.

When Cloud had whickered, sensing it was her, not Heidi, under the cape, she'd almost frozen in shock, waiting for Heston to shout, 'Cut!' But he didn't. Perhaps he'd been impatient to finish filming. Perhaps he'd thought it added extra drama to the scene. Perhaps he'd planned to dub over it during editing. Poppy never found out. But the cameras kept rolling, and she kept her head down as John Manly gave her a leg up and handed her Cloud's reins.

Cloud had needed no encouragement as she'd whirled him around and nudged him with her heels. He'd flown into a gallop, his hooves spraying gravel as he thundered past the side of the house.

As they'd rounded the corner, the wind had blown her hood off, and Poppy thought she'd heard someone exclaim in surprise. But it could have been the squawk of a slumbering rook as they'd raced towards the moor.

Charlie and Scarlett had left the gate open as planned. Cloud galloped through, his grey legs a blur as he widened the distance between them and Claydon Manor. Crouching low over his neck, Poppy was grateful for the clear sky, the waxing moon and the fact that the Connemara was as surefooted as the native

Dartmoor ponies who watched curiously as they flew past.

When she judged they were far enough away, she sat back in the saddle and squeezed the reins. Cloud slowed to a walk and Poppy let the reins slide through her fingers.

'We did it,' she whispered, lacing her fingers in his mane and smiling into the night. 'We'll soon be home.'

Cloud stopped, threw his head up and whinnied. And that's when Poppy heard it. The unmistakeable beating of hooves. And they were coming towards them.

33

C loud spun around, almost unseating Poppy, and her grip on his mane tightened. 'It's all right,' she soothed. 'It's only a Dartmoor pony.' She ran a hand along his neck and squinted into the gloom.

Cloud whinnied, the sound unnaturally loud in the stillness of a Dartmoor night. An answering whinny, like an echo, made Poppy's blood run cold. Instinct told her it was too deep to be a Dartmoor pony. The moon disappeared behind a cloud as Poppy dithered. And then it popped back out, casting its silvery light on a powerful black horse that was galloping at full pelt towards them.

Isadore.

Even from this distance Poppy could see the whites of the black stallion's eyes. Her gaze drifted higher. Blonde hair glinted in the moonlight. It took a second for the realisation to sink in, but when it did her jaw dropped. The rider on Isadore's back was Krystal. The same woman who'd claimed to have been paralysed in a riding accident yet had admitted the previous day that she could walk. And here she was, galloping towards them, her body low and lithe over Isadore's neck as she urged him faster. Had it all been a lie?

Poppy didn't have time to wonder, because Isadore was approaching fast. She had seconds to make a decision. Stand her ground or flee. Fight or flight. Her heart crashing in her ribcage, she turned Cloud towards home and urged him on.

Isadore was almost a couple of hands higher than Cloud, and on a smooth grassy track would have been the faster horse by a country mile. But this was Dartmoor, Cloud's home turf. Isadore may have been fast, but he wasn't used to the uneven terrain. Fleet-footed and nimble, Cloud seemed to sense obstacles before he reached them, swerving to avoid granite boulders with the grace of a top-flight gymkhana pony and soaring over narrow streams like a Grand Prix showjumper. Poppy, who trusted him with her life, gave him his head.

Behind her, just audible above the pounding of the horses' hooves and the whistle of the wind, was Krystal's voice, driving Isadore faster. Poppy glanced over her shoulder, her heart lurching as she realised they were gaining on them.

Where should they go? Home was due east, but the going was easier, and Isadore would in all likelihood catch up with them. Poppy pictured the landscape as Cloud galloped on. Hickman's Wood, reputed to be the most haunted place on Dartmoor, was to their north.

An ancient swathe of gnarly, stunted, lichen-covered oak trees, it resembled an enchanted forest in a Tolkien story. The trees grew so close together they intertwined in places, and Poppy and Cloud always made a beeline for them in the height of summer. Even when the temperatures were sweltering, the woods were cool and shady.

The woods were crisscrossed with narrow paths which weaved through the trees like tangled ribbons. Poppy and Scarlett had once given Georgia and her friends the slip in Hickman's Wood. Poppy was sure she and Cloud could lose Krystal.

Shifting her weight in the saddle, she squeezed her left rein. If Cloud wondered why they were changing direction, he didn't pause to question it. Not for the first time she marvelled at his unshakeable faith in her. If only she had the same belief in herself.

A low stone wall surrounded the wood. If they veered west, they could gallop straight in through an old gateway. But if they kept on course, they could jump the wall and disappear into the trees before Krystal realised they'd gone.

Decision made, Poppy checked Cloud, easing him into a canter. She risked another look over her shoulder. Picking his way through a rocky outcrop, Isadore had slowed, too. As Poppy watched, he stumbled, throwing Krystal forwards in the saddle. But she righted herself almost immediately and yelled at him to look where he was going.

Five strides before the wall, the moon disappeared behind another cloud, turning the world black, and for a moment Cloud faltered. And then Krystal swore loudly behind them, and the Connemara surged forwards.

One. Two. Poppy counted the strides in her head. *Three.* The moon reappeared, lighting their way. *Four. Five.* Cloud launched himself into the air, clearing the low wall by half a metre or more. Landing neatly on the springy grass, he galloped on through the trees.

And then Poppy heard a sound that would stay with her forever. A bloodcurdling scream, more piercing than a vixen's cry.

And then, more eerily still, total silence.

34

Cloud stopped in his tracks and whipped around so they were facing the way they'd come. Ears pricked, he stared into the darkness and whinnied. An answering whinny from Isadore assured Poppy that he was all right, at least. She cocked her head, listening for Krystal. But apart from the whistle of the wind through the trees, there was no sound.

Poppy knew that if they went now, they'd be home inside thirty minutes. She pictured herself leading Cloud up the Riverdale drive and back to safety, his ordeal over. Charlie and Scarlett would already be home, and although Caroline would have rumbled their plan to expose the purse thief, she'd be glad they'd rescued Cloud.

Someone on the set of Black Beauty would realise their horse master was missing and eventually they'd send out a search party. Krystal would be found and taken back to Claydon Manor. No harm done.

Making up her mind, Poppy turned Cloud for home. But they hadn't gone more than half a dozen strides when she halted him and growled in frustration.

'It's no good. I can't go without checking they're OK.' Cloud flicked an ear back. 'One quick look and we'll be on our way,' she promised.

As they neared the wall Poppy could make out the shadow of a riderless horse through the gloom. Isadore was standing behind the wall, his reins hanging loose and his flanks heaving. One of his stirrup leathers was missing. What if Krystal had lost her balance, fallen and been dragged along behind him? With a creeping sense of dread, Poppy nudged Cloud on.

'Krystal?' she said, her voice shaky with fear. 'Are you OK?'

Nothing.

She cleared her throat and tried again, louder this time. 'Krystal! Are you all right?'

A faint moan reached her ears. So quiet that at first Poppy assumed it was the wind sighing in the trees. But when the next groan was followed by a string of muttered expletives, relief washed through her. Krystal was alive, and Poppy could head home, her conscience intact.

'Call an ambulance. I can't feel my legs!' Krystal's voice cut through the soupy darkness, making Poppy jump.

Her eyebrows shot up. Krystal was talking nonsense. She must have bumped her head when she fell.

'You're paralysed. Of course you can't feel your legs,' she said.

'I have limited mobility, but I'm not paralysed. I wasn't, anyway.' A deranged laugh ricocheted through the trees. 'Wouldn't that be the ultimate irony? Pretend to be in a wheelchair and actually end up in one?'

Poppy jumped off Cloud and led him closer to Isadore. The two horses touched noses and Poppy peered over the wall.

'I'm over here,' Krystal said impatiently. 'Call an ambulance or give me your phone and I'll do it.'

Krystal was leaning against a large boulder, her legs splayed motionless in front of her. She groaned again, her hands on her face. 'Just give me your damn phone!'

Satisfied the horse master wasn't in immediate danger, Poppy shook her head. 'Not until you give me your word you won't take Cloud to Yorkshire.'

'Who told you I was, Ned?'

Poppy was silent.

'That's why you pulled your little stunt.' Krystal laughed again. 'You were wasting your time. I don't need him.'

'But Ned said you couldn't find another pony to play Merrylegs.'

'Ned may think he knows what's going on, sneaking around the place listening in on other people's conversations, but he only heard half the story. I did find another pony. Turns out a trainer I've worked with in the past imports horses from the same stud in Ireland that I've been using for years. He has Perry's full brother. And he's a fully-trained stunt horse, not like your happy little hacker.'

'Happy hacker?' Poppy bristled. 'He did his best for you, even though you starved him and exercised him until he was exhausted. Ned showed me a video of you cranking a horse's head high and leaving him tied up all night just so he'd be easy to train the next day. It's despicable.' The memory of the footage sent her pulse soaring, furious indignation pounding through her veins. 'Anna Sewell wrote Black Beauty to encourage people to be kind to horses. And yet you... you...' she spluttered, 'you think it's acceptable to abuse them to get them to do what you want. *That's* the ultimate irony.'

'I'm no worse than the showjumper who gets his grooms to raise a pole to rap his horse's legs so he jumps higher, or the trainers who use soring on Tennessee walking horses to make them lift their legs. What about the riders who push their horses to the limits in endurance races in the Middle East? Are they better or worse than people who dope racehorses or use harsh bits on horses with sensitive mouths? The end game is the same - an obedient horse that does its job. Everyone's at it.'

'Just because other people do it doesn't mean it's right,' Poppy cried.

'Yeah, yeah, whatever.' Krystal held out her hand. 'Phone.'

'And that's another thing. How could you lead people to believe you're paralysed when you're clearly not? I bet you didn't even have a riding accident.'

Krystal glared at Poppy. 'I had an accident all right. I shattered four vertebrae in my back and injured my spinal cord. After surgery and four months on a rehabilitation ward, I could walk with crutches. But crutches don't make you a hero, they're a sign of weakness. A wheelchair, however...' Krystal's voice trailed off.

'A wheelchair what?' Poppy said in morbid fascination.

'Train horses from a wheelchair, and suddenly you're brave and fearless, a warrior. Everyone involved in the media and film industry loves a dramatic backstory. The ultimate hero's journey. When I started training horses again, journalists were falling over themselves to interview me, and directors were lining up to hire me. Why would I want to be just another run-of-the-mill horse master when I could be the legendary Krystal King, defying the odds to train the best stunt horses in the country from her wheelchair?'

Krystal shifted on the ground and gasped in pain. Poppy's hand tightened around her phone.

'Did you know Ned was the purse thief?' she said.

Krystal grunted. 'Thought he might be. Always skulking around. Caught him ferreting through the drawers in my lorry once. Claimed he was looking for a hoof pick. And he had form.'

'What d'you mean? He said he stole the stuff because he wanted to get away from you.'

Krystal's bark of laughter turned into a cough, and she clutched her sides and inhaled sharply. 'Did he tell you I was the only one to offer him a job when he left the Young Offender Institution? No, I didn't think so. He'd served six months for petty theft. Shoplifting, stealing phones and purses, that kind of thing. He'd been on the dole for a year when I took him on. Funny way to repay me.'

Poppy swallowed. 'At least he wasn't cruel to the horses.'

The older woman snorted. 'He didn't have a problem following my orders.'

'He didn't have a choice!'

Somewhere in the trees, an owl hooted, and Poppy shivered. Krystal thought it was acceptable to mistreat horses to get results. Ned thought it was perfectly reasonable to help himself to other people's hard-earned belongings. They were as corrupt as each other. Suddenly all she wanted was to get as far away from both of them as possible.

'I'll phone an ambulance and tell them where you are. After that, I'm taking Cloud home,' she said.

'Wait.' Krystal held out a hand. 'What will you do with that footage?'

Weariness hit Poppy like a battering ram, and she leant on Cloud in case her legs buckled beneath her.

'I'll be sending it to the RSPCA first thing tomorrow. I'm afraid the game's up, Krystal. You should have taken a leaf out of Anna Sewell's book. You can't treat horses like that.'

35

R iverdale was in darkness as Poppy jumped off Cloud and led him through the gate into the stable yard. Chester hee-hawed and, as the security light flicked on, the old donkey's chocolate brown nose appeared over his stable door, closely followed by Jenny's.

He'd known, Poppy thought, as she ran up the stirrup leathers and unfastened Cloud's girth. Poppy, who loved Cloud with all her heart, hadn't seen the danger signs. But Chester, through some uncanny sixth sense, had.

By the time she'd untacked Cloud, brushed him down and fixed his stable rug, she heard the familiar sound of their estate car trundling up the drive. Doors slammed, the engine cut out, and footsteps pounded around the side of the house.

Charlie appeared first, his eyes wide.

'You're home!' he cried. 'It's all right, Mum, she's here,' he yelled over his shoulder.

Caroline was next to appear. Her face broke into a smile when she saw Poppy. 'Thank goodness. We've been so worried.'

Finally, Scarlett burst around the corner. She ran over to Poppy and waved something in her face. 'Look, my phone! I've got it back!'

Poppy grinned. 'You'll be able to be a social influencer after all.'

'No freakin' way. I'll stick with obscurity, thanks.' Scarlett peered at Poppy. 'You both OK?'

'We're fine.'

Charlie tugged her sleeve. 'Mum says we're not in trouble.'

'Not in too much trouble,' Caroline corrected him, shaking her head. 'I think we've all had enough excitement for one night. I don't know about the rest of you, but I could do with a cup of tea.'

Once they were settled around the kitchen table with mugs in front of them, Charlie rubbed his hands together. 'We want to know exactly what happened. Every single second of it.'

'First, I want to know what happened when Cloud and I galloped off,' Poppy told him.

'All hell let loose,' he crowed.

'Everyone thought Cloud had bolted and Heidi couldn't stop him,' Scarlett said. 'I heard Krystal muttering something about her being a rubbish rider.'

'Heidi heard Krystal, too,' Charlie chortled. 'You should have seen her face.'

'She was watching?'

He nodded. 'From the doorway. No-one noticed

her because they were too busy staring after you and Cloud.'

'Heston was fuming,' Scarlett said. 'He turned on Krystal and yelled, "It's not my actress that's the problem, it's your flipping horse! Call yourself a horse master?"'

'Ouch,' Poppy said with feeling.

'Krystal was incandescent with rage. You could almost feel it coming off her in waves,' Scarlett continued.

Charlie nodded. 'It gave her superhuman powers because you'll never guess what happened next.'

'She got out of her wheelchair and jumped onto Isadore without any help?'

Charlie's eyes widened. 'How did you guess?'

'She admitted to me that she's not paralysed at all. She has problems walking, sure, but she only uses the wheelchair for the sympathy vote.'

'Crikey,' he said, his eyes growing rounder.

'Anyway, Krystal was sitting on Isadore when she looked back at the house and saw Heidi standing there, cool as a cucumber. And she screamed, literally screamed, "I knew it!" and galloped off after you,' Scarlett said. 'That's when everyone else realised it wasn't Heidi riding Cloud after all. But before Heston spontaneously combusted Heidi whipped out her phone and showed him the footage of that poor horse. He was furious, but not with us. He said Krystal had not only put him in an impossible position, but she'd also jeopardised the whole production.'

Caroline refilled the teapot and topped up their mugs. 'That's when I turned up.'

Seeing Poppy's confusion, she explained, 'Pat phoned to ask if I could send Scarlett home with the coffee and walnut cake recipe. I told her I'd sent you and Charlie over with it earlier. It didn't take long for us to put two and two together and realise we'd been hoodwinked. I guessed you'd gone to see Cloud, so I headed to Claydon Manor.' Her forehead puckered and she looked from Poppy to Charlie and back again. 'You must both promise never to lie to me again.'

Charlie nodded, his eyes downcast.

'Don't be cross with Charlie. It was my idea, and I'm truly sorry,' Poppy said. 'But I knew you'd never let us go and I had to get Cloud out of there.'

'I understand why you did it. But that doesn't mean I approve,' Caroline said, waggling a finger at them.

'Sorry,' they chimed.

'Apology accepted.'

'Then we heard sirens, and an ambulance came tearing up the drive,' Scarlett said. 'The driver said they'd had a call to an injured rider and asked the way to Hickman's Wood.'

'Did you call them?' Charlie asked Poppy.

She nodded, then giggled. 'I should have the emergency services on speed dial.'

Caroline shook her head in despair. 'I was worried it was you.'

'They had to go on foot because they couldn't drive the ambulance across the moor, so we went with them to show them the way.' Charlie grinned. 'They let me carry one end of the stretcher.'

'Cool.'

'And we found Krystal by the entrance to the wood, just as you'd told them,' Scarlett said.

'Of course, you were nowhere in sight. But I assumed you'd ridden home. I knew Cloud would look after you,' Caroline said.

'He did.' Poppy smiled at the memory. As they'd ambled back across the moonlit moor she'd felt at peace for the first time since Cloud had left Riverdale. 'I had to bring him home. I didn't want him around that Krystal woman another second.' She chewed her bottom lip. 'Was she all right?'

'They put her on a spinal board just in case she'd damaged her back, but the paramedic didn't think it was too serious as she was starting to get feeling back in her legs.'

'That's good, I guess,' Poppy said.

'If this was a book, she'd have got her just desserts and would have been forced to use a wheelchair for the rest of her miserable life.'

'Scarlett!' Caroline spluttered.

Scarlett shrugged. 'It's no more than she deserves. Oh, and I got to ride Isadore back to his stable.'

'Double cool.' Poppy yawned so widely her jaw clicked.

'You're shattered,' Caroline said. 'Pat said Scarlett can sleep here tonight. Let's get you all up to bed.'

'But Poppy hasn't told us what happened to her and Cloud,' Charlie said.

'They'll be plenty of time for that in the morning. Bed. Now!'

Poppy and Scarlett put the camp bed together under Charlie's exacting gaze, and Caroline found spare bedding. Pulling a clean pair of pyjamas from the airing cupboard, Poppy handed them to Scarlett.

'They aren't My Little Pony ones, I'm afraid. Will they do?'

'I haven't worn them for years,' Scarlett scoffed. 'They'll do fine.'

Poppy sighed as she snuggled into bed.

'Oh dear, what's up?'

'It's been a long day. A long two weeks. And I've just remembered we're back to school on Monday. What a waste of the Easter holidays. We didn't get to do any of the things we'd planned.'

'But we got to be extras in a TV show. That was fun, even if it did have its moments. And we're friends with a famous actress.'

'Not that famous,' Poppy muttered before she could stop herself.

Scarlett rolled her eyes. 'She will be when Black Beauty hits our screens. So will Cloud. Are you sure you don't want to set up an Instagram account for him?'

'Absolutely one hundred per cent sure. I don't want him becoming public property. He's mine, and that's the way it's going to stay. And I'm never going to let him out of my sight again. I've learnt my lesson.'

'Oh yeah, what's that?'

'Fame comes at a price I'm not prepared to pay.'

Scarlett snorted. 'That's a bit self-righteous.'

Poppy laughed, too. 'You're right, it does sound a bit pompous. OK then, this whole thing has taught me that I'd rather have a common or garden, everyday kind of a pony than some celebrity pony who everyone wants a piece of. Because d'you know what?'

'What?' Scarlett said.

Poppy could hear the smile in her best friend's voice, and she smiled, too. 'I've realised I don't care what other people think. Cloud doesn't need to be famous because he'll always be a superstar in my eyes, and that's what matters.'

36

Caroline was serving bacon sandwiches the following morning when there was a rap at the front door. Freddie woofed, jumped out of his bed and scampered along the hall.

'I'll go,' Charlie said, shovelling a triangle of toast into his mouth.

'Wipe the ketchup off your chin first,' Caroline called as he raced out of the kitchen.

The door slammed, and Charlie said, 'She's in here.' The crackle of a police radio sent a shiver up Poppy's spine, and she pushed her plate away and licked her lips. What were the police doing here so soon? What if they'd dusted Ned's swag bag and found her finger-prints all over it? Were they here to arrest her for theft, handcuff her, march her to the nearest police cell, lock the door and throw away the key?

Before her thoughts spiralled further, Charlie and Freddie burst into the room, followed by PC Claire Bodiam.

'Bacon sandwich?' Caroline asked, placing a plate in front of the officer before she had a chance to answer.

PC Bodiam nodded her thanks and turned down the volume of her radio so it was no louder than the fizz of a newly-opened can of cola.

'Poppy,' she said, not meeting Poppy's eye. *Bad sign.* 'I'm glad you're here.'

'What's up?' Caroline said, passing her a mug of tea.

PC Bodiam wrapped her fingers around the mug and blew her fringe out of her eyes. 'I wanted to update Poppy on some recent developments in my investigation.'

Poppy shot a desperate look at Scarlett, who mouthed, 'Don't worry.'

'We had a call from See Red Production's assistant director last night. Seems as though the stolen goods have been located.' PC Bodiam finally looked Poppy in the eye. 'He said you'd found them by the Portaloos.'

'I did, but I didn't…'

The officer held up a hand to silence her. 'I went straight over, and we checked them for fingerprints. Yours were all over them.'

Poppy's heart sank. She rolled up her sleeves, ready to hold out her wrists so PC Bodiam could slap on the handcuffs.

'But we also found another set of prints. A set that belongs to a certain Edward Plover, a petty criminal from Hertfordshire.'

'Where's that?' Charlie asked.

'It doesn't matter,' Caroline said, patting his shoulder.

'Mr Plover's modus operandi is to steal purses, jewellery and the like from people's places of work,' PC Bodiam continued. 'He searches through bags and pockets and helps himself. But he moved out of Hert-fordshire a while back when he got a job in Hampshire. He told his probation officer he wanted a fresh start. Unfortunately, it seems his light-fingered ways were too deeply ingrained for him to turn over a new leaf.'

Things were slowly making sense and Poppy risked a look at the police officer.

'Are Edward Plover and Krystal's Ned one and the same?'

PC Bodiam nodded. 'They are indeed. Plover was picked up by a patrol car trying to hitch a lift on the A30 early this morning. He's admitted twelve counts of theft and is likely to appear before magistrates before the end of the week.'

'He only took the stuff because he had to get away from Krystal,' Poppy said.

Scarlett's jaw dropped. 'Are you sticking up for him?'

'Of course not. I just thought PC Bodiam ought to know.'

'He'll have a chance to speak to a solicitor and put forward his side of the story. I'm sure the magistrates will take his situation into account when he's sentenced,' the officer said.

'And what about Krystal?' Caroline asked. 'Has anyone shown you the footage of her so-called training methods?'

'See Red's assistant director sent it to me last night,'

PC Bodiam said. 'I've passed it to my contact at the RSPCA. She'll make sure Ms King is investigated thoroughly.'

'Will she be jailed?' Poppy asked.

'Potentially, yes. She could also receive a ban on keeping animals. And once word gets out…'

'No other production company's going to touch her with a bargepole,' Scarlett said with satisfaction.

A thought struck Poppy. 'What'll happen to Perry and Isadore and all her other horses?'

'The RSPCA will take care of them, don't you worry about that,' PC Bodiam said.

'I wonder if they'll even be able to finish filming,' Caroline mused.

'Who knows?' PC Bodiam drained her mug. 'I'd best be off. We've had reports of salmon poachers down at Combe Falls. But before I go there's one final thing I need to give Poppy.'

Poppy looked up sharply.

The officer held up her hands and shrugged her shoulders. 'An apology. I'm sorry I may have come across as heavy-handed, even a bit Draconian. I didn't believe for one minute that you'd stolen anything, but I had to investigate thoroughly. I also wanted you to realise that you can't just take the law into your own hands, because sooner or later you're going to land yourself in hot water.'

'It's OK, I understand. And you were only doing your job.'

PC Bodiam dipped her head, and her mouth twitched. 'You'll be pleased to hear I've officially ruled you out of my inquiries. But if I ever, *ever*, catch you playing detective again there'll be trouble.'

Poppy grinned and laid a hand on her heart. 'You have my word. No more detective work, I promise.'

'We promise, too, don't we Scarlett?' Charlie said, clutching his heart with his right hand.

Scarlett nodded, mirroring them both.

'Progress!' PC Bodiam said to Caroline, who raised an eyebrow.

'We'll see.' She pushed her chair back. 'I'll see you to the door.'

The three children were silent as the police officer gathered her radio and notebook and disappeared out of the room after Caroline. When their footsteps died away, Charlie whipped his left hand out from behind his back.

'Oops,' he said, staring at his crossed fingers.

Scarlett was next to show them the firmly-crossed index finger and middle finger of her left hand. 'It was a big ask,' she said reproachfully.

They both turned to Poppy.

'Well?' they said in unison.

Poppy shifted in her seat. PC Bodiam was probably right. Playing detective could land them in a whole stinking muckheap of trouble. But it was what they did best. How could they stand by and do nothing when there were mysteries to solve, wrongs to right, and adventures to be had?

Infinitesimally slowly, she produced her left hand. Not only were her index and middle fingers crossed, but her little and ring fingers were entwined, too.

Charlie whooped, and Scarlett clapped.

'We should at least try to keep our promise,' Poppy said, her voice solemn.

'Of course,' Charlie said.

'Goes without saying,' Scarlett added.

Poppy inspected her hand and grinned. 'This is insurance, just in case we can't.'

AFTERWORD

Thank you for reading *Edge of Danger*. If you enjoyed this book it would be great if you could spare a couple of minutes to write a quick review on Amazon. I'd love to hear your feedback!

ACKNOWLEDGMENTS

One of the best things about being an author is connecting with people who enjoy reading your stories as much as you enjoy writing them.

Since The Lost Pony of Riverdale was first published in 2013, Poppy, Cloud and the gang have acquired a small army of loyal fans who make writing the Riverdale books an absolute joy. Thank you so much - you have no idea what your support means to me!

Most of all, I would like to thank my small but trusty team of beta readers: Claire Mill, Elizabeth Winterbourne, Anne Collingridge, Pauline Cowell, Sue McDine, and Kate Gordon.

You are amazing and I'm so grateful that you agreed to come along for the ride!

ABOUT THE AUTHOR

Amanda Wills is the Amazon bestselling author of The Riverdale Pony Stories, which follow the adventures of pony-mad Poppy McKeever and her beloved Connemara Cloud.

She is also the author of the Mill Farm Stables series of pony books and Flick Henderson and the Deadly Game, a fast-paced mystery about a super-cool new heroine who has her sights set on becoming an investigative journalist.

Amanda, a UK-based former journalist and police press officer, lives in Kent with her husband and fellow indie author Adrian Wills and their sons Oliver and Thomas.

Find out more at www.amandawills.co.uk or at www.facebook.com/riverdaleseries or follow amandawillsauthor on Instagram.

THE FLICK HENDERSON FILES

Flick Henderson and the Deadly Game

Printed in Great Britain
by Amazon